One Day in the Life of a Born Again Loser
and Other Stories

A Deep South Book

One Day in the Life of a Born Again Loser

AND OTHER STORIES

Helen Norris

THE UNIVERSITY OF ALABAMA PRESS
TUSCALOOSA

1 2 3 4 5 6 7 8 9 . 07 06 05 04 03 02 01 00

Design by Shari DeGraw

The author acknowledges the original publication of the following: "Judgment Day," *The Southern Review* 27, no. 3, new series (Summer 1991); "The Flying Hawk," *The Southern Review* 29, no. 1, new series (Winter 1993); "A Good Shape," *Boulevard* 4, no. 2 (Fall 1989), edited by Richard Burgin; "One Day in the Life of a Born Again Loser," *Western Humanities Review* 37, no. 1 (Spring 1983).

The paper on which this book is printed meets the minimum requirements of American National Standard for Information Science – Permanence of Paper for Printed Library Materials,
ANSI Z39.48 – 1984.

Library of Congress Cataloging-in-Publication Date

Norris, Helen, 1916–
One day in the life of a born again loser, and other stories / Helen Norris.
p. cm.
"Deep South Books."
ISBN 0-8173-1029-0 (alk. paper)
1. Southern States—Social life and customs—Fiction. I. Title.
PS3527.O497 O54 2000
813'.52—dc21   99-006957

For my mother and father,
who loved a good tale
and read Victor Hugo on their honeymoon

Contents

The Bower-Bird

THUNDER CRACKED A WHIP in the west. In a thunderstorm you weren't to phone. He thought that if it was going to storm he'd make the call before it did.

Someone answered the phone at once. A woman's voice with a breathy quality, rather sweet. When he told his name and asked for Joe, she kept him waiting. "We were in Nam," he offered at last, trying with patience to read her silence. "This is the last address I have."

He had crashed for the night at an inn of sorts, where now he stretched on a sagging bed. The air of his room was sagging, awaiting rain. Under his shoulder were papers for the interview that had led to nothing and now lay scattered over the spread. In the bed light above him a resident insect warmed and sang.

Now she was back and asking him, "What did you say your name was?"

"Will Geer." He spelled it for her. "This is the last address I have."

He heard her speaking in hushed tones. She returned to him. "I'm sorry to tell you my brother is dead."

He took it in, but not at once, letting it settle into him — the way your mother had covered you so as not to wake you in the night, the way, when you jumped and hit the ground, the parachute came down on you, as if you had plunged below the ground and waited for earth to shut you in — and while the words were settling, he said he was sorry and asked her when.

There was always the feeling back in Nam — they'd talked about it on river patrol — that if you made it through the war, you figured you'd never have to die. It was a sobering thing to hear. That Joe was dead? Or to find that after all they were wrong? He told her again that he was sorry, that it had been six or seven years, maybe eight, since he'd been in touch. He tried to recall if Joe had ever mentioned a sister. Perhaps by now he'd acquired a wife.

"When did it happen?" he asked again. When didn't matter, but it was something you had to say.

"A year ago." Again she was speaking in hushed tones. She was back with him. "My mother would like you to come to supper."

He said at once, "I'm on my way back to Tennessee. I was here on business overnight and wanted to call before I left."

"She says she wants it very much. A friend of Joseph's. Just to talk." There was a pause. "And of course your wife . . . if she is here."

"No wife," he said.

"Please come," she said. "We both want it so very much."

It was the last thing he wanted, of course. He toyed with refusal. He groaned and said he would like to come.

He was wishing to God he hadn't called. Funny the way it was with Nam. Home, he wanted to wipe it out. And then he wanted to be with them, with some one who could bring it back. And when it was back he drowned in it and had to run and later on to get it back. You were something like a rubber band. You pulled away and you snapped back.

He listened to rain invading the land, the rising wind, the thrashing trees, and then the buckshot against the pane. The war was a long, long time ago, and Joe was buckshot against the pane.

He and Joe hadn't been close at first. But it was amazing how close you got when bullets were flying over your head. The fear was like an undertow that swept you down and out to sea. You clung to anyone around. And after the fear was at an end, you kept in touch in a sort of way. The fear had opened up your brain. The guy was there inside your brain. And you were there inside his brain. That was the kind of close it was. And if he was dead . . . well, he was still inside your brain, and what was different was that now you weren't in his. The last thing of all he wanted to do was face Joe's sister and, God, his mother and try to come up with something to say.

He packed his bag for checking out. After he'd managed the supper thing, he'd leave at once and drive all night.

The rain thinned and abruptly stopped. It was early September. Summer was ripe and ready to fall. He drove through streets that were tired of it. He saw it in the listless trees. It was, as she'd said, not hard to find. A shopping center was cropped to galleries, then to cloisters. And it was there beyond a gate among the elms, a large brick building, two stories of it, old with a smudge of the city upon it. The bricks, once white, had weathered into a mottled red. They lived, she had said, in the downstairs part.

She took so long to answer his knock that almost he had turned away. Then she was there, a small woman in long, full skirt and peasant blouse, the waist clipped in with a fringed red scarf, the dark hair coiled and caught behind with a smaller, matching scarf. The face was pale and almost pretty, with pale but animated eyes, and reddened lips. He took the hand that was offered to him. It had an almost feverish warmth. He felt old for his forty-three years, in need of a shave, in need of a job; he was sure it showed and did not care. He guessed she was thirty-eight, or more. He didn't care.

"The friend of Joseph is welcome," she said in the voice that was breathy and almost sweet. She gave him a modest little smile that gathered force, till he dropped his own. Let's get it over, he wanted to say.

He followed her into a small parlor, the kind his great-grandmother had had, with a dark that put a curse on you. A cord from a fixture overhead fell straight to a lamp with an amber shade shaped, he thought, like a quonset hut. It stood in the center of a round table with a cluster of objects it faintly lit. Beside them a frail and elderly woman sat in a wheelchair awaiting him. The amber light was in her hair, a pewter gray and deeply ridged like a ploughed field. He was fairly sure that she wore a wig. It framed a sharp, unyielding face. She stared at him with baleful eyes.

"You knew my son?" He caught the challenge in her voice.

"Yes, ma'am," he said, "we were in Nam."

"He always called it Viet Nam."

"Yes, ma'am," he said.

"Everything gets cropped," she said. "Snipped off. People have to get on with it. Words are snipped, names are snipped, then your life. I suppose your name was snipped from 'William.'"

"No, ma'am," he said, "I was born Will."

"He never mentioned you," she said.

But the younger woman broke in at that. "Yes, he did. He spoke of Will."

Her mother listened imperiously. "Did you volunteer for the war?" she asked.

"No, ma'am," he said, and after a moment, "No, I didn't."

"It was a stupid waste," she said. "You may as well sit down." She sighed and turned a little in her chair, as if having seen him, she would leave.

He did not know what to make of her. He had thought he was there at her request.

The younger woman was beckoning him. "We planned to eat in the garden," she said. "It's pleasant now and not too damp. The rain has freshened the air a bit." She smiled at him as if her mother's curious welcome left nothing at all to be explained. She turned and with a swift gesture, she parted what proved to be double doors and he could see what she called the garden.

She beckoned him again to follow. He glanced around at the older woman. She had turned her chair into shadow, but he felt her eyes upon him still.

The younger woman was waiting for him. "Call me Tina if you will. Joseph always called me that. It will be nice to hear it from you."

Small and close, locked in with shrubs, the garden reminded him of the parlor. In the waning light of the afternoon, it was filled with shadows cast by leaves, by clouds which still were on the prowl. The branch of an elm tree dripped with rain. On the plot of grass there was scarcely room for the folding table. He saw there were places set for four.

She sat him down on a metal bench, which first she dried with the fringe of the scarf that clipped her waist. She made a playful task of it, finally drying it with her hand. Rings on her fingers winked with light. She came and went with supper food. In the limited space they were very close. It made him think of the boat in Nam, the way the jungle jammed you in, till you seemed to dream another's dream and he was likely dreaming yours. Things the river made you dream. River dreams in the light of day. Dreams of home with a river haze and a danger smell. At night you never slept to dream. You closed your eyes and went on with it, the waiting, the watching. You woke with your eyes worn out with the scene. It was easy to call it up again. He closed his eyes and was watching her and wanting to be away from her and down the road, away from her. He gave it up and opened them.

He saw that she walked with a slight limp. The damp grass would brush her skirt where her left foot dipped into its rain. As it swept the shrubs, the red scarf about her waist grew ever darker with their wet. Beneath the embroidered sleeves of her blouse her bare arms faintly glowed with it. She appeared to be preoccupied, but he felt her keenly aware of him. She circled the table, making arrangements, shifting things, weaving him into her presence there. He could not escape the soft, hypnotic scent she wore. Nor could he think of a thing to say.

The afternoon was beginning to pale. The highway traffic sound grew shrill, like a long cry from a distant hill. Suddenly she turned to him. "Remember, it's Tina. It will make me happy if Joseph's friend will call me that."

"I will," he said.

As if from a sign, the old lady wheeled herself into the yard and smoothly parked herself at the table. She seemed to have dropped her hostility. She now was affable, even gracious. As she chewed her food with a pensive air, her eyes, narrowed and dark with guile, rested upon the empty place. She talked of former days in the city, how all was altered, not for the best. Each remark was heralded with a rounded sweep of her delicate hand and sealed with yet another sweep. But once in protesting a recent change, she made a fist that enclosed her fork and struck the table with its base. Like an unruly child, he thought. Like prisoners they took in Nam beating their fists for want of words with which to make frustration known. But she was not in want of words. The talk was hers. The daughter served them in silence, her lip caught in a little smile.

He half expected a tardy guest, another relative, perhaps, to take the place that was set for him.

It surprised him to find he was hungry. The food was prepared with skill, he thought. Something fish, with a spiciness. His glass was filled several times with wine. Its fruitiness had an edge to it, but as he drank, his palate found it even smooth, till at last his mood had matched the wine. The voice of the woman receded. He had braced himself for the talk of Joe, but nothing was said of Joe or Nam. He seemed to be any visitor. He could almost believe he was gone from there and eating somewhere down the road, and the girl with a pencil in her hair came and removed the empty place, the knife and fork, whatever else, because there was no one to be there. By now it was clear there would never be.

Tree frogs came to life in the shrubs. A fragment of moon was in the sky. A cloudy breath of spider nets, woven together with drops of rain, was visible now on leaf and branch. The old lady fell silent, dark and motionless as a spider waiting at the edge of her web. Abruptly she laid down her glass and wheeled herself from the table. "Tina will see to you," she said. With an upward, rounded thrust of her hand, she disappeared through the folding doors.

They sat in silence in her wake. At length he asked: "Was there someone who didn't come?"

She took a little sip of her wine. "We set a place for Joseph. Perhaps it seems a little strange. Mother likes it done that way."

He drained his glass. "Why not?" he said.

The small enclosure became oppressive. The foliage, grayed in the failing light, seemed to advance to wall them in. Since Nam he had never been easy with this — with vegetation that hemmed him in. He wanted to be on the highway, but he found it hard to make the move, to say, well, this is all there is. Whatever I had to say to Joe . . . but I didn't have anything to say. If he'd been sitting here tonight, we probably wouldn't have said a thing. We'd have dropped Nam on the table there and looked at it without a word.

Her face was smiling in the dusk. Fireflies came and struck her hair. With a swift gesture she captured one, then another, and then a third, and tipped them into her wine glass. She covered it with her little hand, the fingers spread to make a wing. Her rings were flickering with light. "Now they belong to me," she said. "They will drink the wine I have left for them, and then they'll forget about leaving me."

She was close to him. Her arms were covered with pearly down. Perhaps she was older than he had thought. The shoulders, he saw, were slightly stooped. The hand that had trapped the fire-flies was delicate and even worn, with the curious kind of trans-lucence that he had seen in the old or ill. She struck him as being . . . perishable. He could not think of another word. The fruit that fell from the trees in Nam, you left it there, for despite its bloom, the bruise it sustained had spread throughout.

He stirred. "I have to be on my way."

"You mustn't yet." She closed her fingers about the glass.

"Was there something about your brother in Nam? Did you want to know about that?" he asked.

"No," she said and held the fireflies to her face. She pressed her lips against the glass.

Before he could rise, she stood for him. "I want you to see my room," she said.

He did not know what to make of that. "I have a good ways to go tonight . . . but I'd like to tell your mother goodbye."

"No, no, my mother has gone to bed. As soon as it's dark she goes to bed. She leaves the visitors to me. I want you to see where I laugh and cry."

She disappeared among the shrubs. "Here," she called, "through the looking-glass." She had slipped toward a rear, protruding wing. The house, he saw, had the shape of an L.

He waited a moment, a long moment. He had never since Nam been easy with entering heavy foliage. Then he followed her

through an evenfall of overarching shrubs and vines, soaked with
rain, thick with the gossamer of webs, alive with birds that had
bedded down. He heard their faint, protesting cries. He found she
had opened a door for him.

A curious room burst into bloom. A light and shadow clutter
of things, oppressive as her garden had been, as if a gathering of
children had played with all the toys they owned and abandoned
them when sent to bed. He could not take it in at once.

She was watching him and laughed aloud. "Well, aren't you glad
you came?" she asked.

For lack of words, he matched her laugh. "Tell me what it is,"
he said.

"I made it, the way God made the world."

"It has so much to see," he said.

She smiled. "The way God made the world."

Bowls were crowded with purple asters, the kind that grew
wild along the road. Above a mantel were crossed swords. There
were lamps of many shapes and heights, some with bright, trans-
lucent shades etched with leaves and butterflies. Statuary, shelves
of books, wall paintings, easels mounted with landscapes, sea-
scapes. A circular tank of colorful fish, a sheltering palm, an al-
mond tree. Filmy draperies, curios. Figurines of gilt and bronze.
Porcelains and colorful glass, garlands of seashells. A velvet hanging with cockatoos, a doorway curtained with crystal beads. Tap-
estries. A bird cage wound with a silver scarf. A golden harp.
Everywhere there were mirrors endlessly repeating the room, till
it echoed for him with a frenzied cry of hue and shine and shifting form.

She went to the cage and unwound the scarf carefully as she
would a shroud; she must not startle the bird to life. The bird was
perched on his tiny swing, his head burrowed in yellow down.

She seated herself before the harp and closed her eyes. The
foliage had loosened her coil of hair. It fell about her face and

throat, dark and full, with a drift of gray. Her skirt was drenched and clung to her. She seemed to be unaware of it.

He stood before her, drenched as well, trapped and listening while she reached across the strings, as if she gathered in the chords, plunging her fingers into gold, catching a chord that had wandered off.

The objects in the cluttered room began to vibrate as she plucked. The crimson fish in the lighted tank fluttered faintly with each chord. The bird awoke and stretched his wing with a tiny chuckle and flung his head. Wind-chimes wailed a fledgling cry.

It began to seem as if she made a single note and the room itself would sound with it. He had heard it said that for Chinamen the sacred river rushing by intoned the *kung* of their music. The mighty rivers, the great cities, the giant forests struck the note. From the boat you heard the jungle — chirrs, cries, and chatterings, moist and full with a listening, longing, stuttering breath; and suddenly the silence fell as if the world dropped dead for you; then if you waited you heard the note. If you died you would walk into the sound, be part of it. Even today and now at night he heard the note and was part of it.

She had placed her wine glass on a table, and now the fireflies rose from it. He watched them circling the room, pricking the shadows with points of light. And then they too timed their lamps to glow whenever she touched the strings.

Her eyes were shut. He had a wild impression they were locked with those of the mother, who waited at the jungle's edge and held the two of them in this room captive in its sound. He thought of escaping the whole of it through the jungle of shrubs and birds, with all the art of a silent passage he still possessed. Now he was on the highway, with the heater on to dry his clothes.

He stood his ground because of one patrol at dusk when the boat plunged through the hanging boughs. He heard the branches

cry and break, the bird's cry, the bullet's cry, and the cry of someone the men called Cap. Not much of a cry, not much of a guy, but
lots of blood.

Her sudden rising shattered it. "I'm going to make you flower
tea. Or coffee?" she asked, lifting her hair with both her hands to
let it fall. She shook it as if it were full of rain.

"Coffee, please. I'll need to stay awake on the road."

"Sit down," she implored.

He glanced at a fragile upholstered chair and raised his hands
in mock despair. "As wet as I am?"

She laughed at him. "No more than I! We'll sit on the floor."

He was conscious of the effort she made. He sensed in her a
weariness that she covered for him with smiling words. She was
the summer ready to fall, the tired streets, the listless trees.

He did not sit till she came to him with his cup and hers. While
he held them both, she brought a rug woven with shining threads.
"This is a prayer rug, I think," she said. "I'm not sure, so we needn't
pray. But do take off your shoes, in case."

He slipped them off. He could not decide if he stood before a
weary child or a woman wise in dalliance.

They sat cross-legged and drank her brew. The old wound in his
thigh awoke. Now on the floor, he had a view of the clutter below
the clutter above — like the jungle floor with its life that was separate from birds and trees — wooden animals curiously carved, the
legs of a table with raven claws. He had once been shown the play-
ground of a bower-bird, how it was decked to lure a mate with bits
of glass, glittering stones, flowers, shells, a colorful thread. At the
end the bird had built a hut, and inside was the nest itself with
berries and flowers replaced each day. He told her of this, for
something to say. She listened to him with too bright a smile, as
if he had wandered too close to her.

"And did the bird get a mate?" she asked.

"I had to move on. I never knew."

"I wish you had waited so you could say."

"It might have taken him a while. Sometimes she has a look and leaves."

"Poor bird. . . . he could have me." Her tone was light, but it struck the wound that throbbed in his thigh. She echoed in him. The way the jungle echoed in him, was in his brain, the way Joe was, as if he had never come home from it. He wanted to rise at once and go. But a lethargy had stolen his limbs. A clock on the far wall opened its door and a golden bird came out and sang. And then the clock began to chime.

"Don't count," she said. "The clock has forgotten all it knew. It is very old and forgets the time."

He waited till the clock was still. "I have to go."

"No," she said, "you will sleep tonight in Joseph's room. He would like that. I'm sure of it."

He stared at her in disbelief and then dismay. Her eyes were as weary as his own. "No," he said.

"Yes," she said. "My mother has set her heart on it." There was entreaty in her voice, an anguish in it that broke his will.

He could not account for his lassitude. It occurred to him she had drugged his coffee. He dismissed the thought. "I can't," he said.

She had risen to her knees. Her full skirt was caressing him, damp but warm with clinging to her. The scent she wore was in his throat. "Why leave tonight? Is it your job . . . or your wife?" she asked.

"I don't have a job or a wife," he said.

"Never a wife?"

"Not since Nam."

"Well, then, of course you have to stay."

Slowly he put on his shoes and knew how tired he had become. He followed her into a narrow hall, then into a room that was simply furnished. It amazed him to find his suitcase there. But he was too weary to question it. He found a bathroom adjoining.

He fell into sleep the way he did. He was always at the jungle's edge. A bird screamed, and then another . . . and then a third that was Cap's scream. And then he entered the dark of the sound, slowly dissolving into sound. He never entered the jungle; instead the jungle entered him.

But in the night he was back in Nam. The particular cry that came from Cap, that gave him sleep and took it back. Almost a cry of joy it was, a child's cry on Christmas morn. And they were slipping in the blood. Joe had turned, come back for him and dragged him below as shots were coming down like rain. One of them got Joe in the arm. I guess I owe you one, he said, and Joe said, Don't forget it, kid.

It wasn't the worst God-awful scene. There were things that could blow his brain to bits. He had let it stand for all the rest, letting it all run into one, and then surrendered himself to it, and that was the way he dealt with Nam. Now he could do it in his sleep . . . guess I owe you one, he said, and Joe said, Don't forget it, kid.

Well, I'm here, he said, swimming out of the scene. I'm here for the night. I ate a meal with a bloody place that was set for you. Is that enough? It wasn't enough. And then he locked the door on Joe, which wasn't the easiest thing to do when he was lying in Joe's bed.

He awoke early, just at dawn. He seemed to be lying with his wife. She'd gone away when he left for Nam. But now, mysteriously, she was back. She must have heard he was home from Nam. I'm out of work, he wanted to say, but now you're back it will be all right. He had only to turn and hold her. It had always been, the dream he had that she was there. All the time he was married to her, she was lying there but not there. Nam had been a long, bad dream, and then for real she wasn't there. Six years of marriage had come to this, dreaming and waking to find her gone.

He showered, shaved, and quickly dressed. The clothes still wet from the night before he rolled and stuffed into his bag. He would get some coffee down the road. But he would not leave without good-bye. He opened the door and all was still. The sun glistened. on shrubs and grass. Birds were chittering overhead. The trucks were shifting, rushing by, as if they rode the darkness down. He found her door and gently knocked. At last she came in a white robe, her hair falling about her face.

"I'm sorry if I woke you," he said, "but I couldn't leave without good-bye. And tell your mother, please, for me."

She opened her door. "Please come in. I was awake. I never sleep. But I dream dreams that are full of things. Like my room they are full of things."

He stepped just inside the door. She seemed to deny there had been a night to break their talk. The fireflies still winked for them.

"Isn't it strange that I can dream and be awake?"

"I do it all the time," he said.

"Are they good dreams?"

"No," he said.

She held his eyes. "My dreams are wonderful," she said. But her eyes clouded and let him go. "If I go to sleep they will slip away. . . . But sometimes I could die for sleep. How wonderful to go to sleep and wake up with your arms full."

She seemed to be asking him for sleep . . . and for the waking he'd never had.

"I'll leave before the road is jammed."

"But no," she said, "you must see Mother."

He was forcibly struck by the change in her. Perhaps his coming and thoughts of her brother had taken their toll of her in the night. Her evening sheen had been brushed away and the dark beneath had been exposed. For an instant he heard the stifled cry that woke his own. . . . The room, bereft of its lamplight, looked a jumble of make-believe, slightly garish in early light, like an aging tart when morning comes and the rouge stands out on her pale face. The roadside asters drooped their heads. The silver scarf that had wound the bird hung like tinsel from the cage.

She smiled at him. "You mustn't see the room like this. It isn't fair. It's still asleep." It seemed to him that she spoke of herself. A change had overtaken him, as if in the night they had spoken words, dream words he could not recall, that had never been spoken in dream at all but bound them all the more for this. In the breaking day she was known to him, as if Joe might have talked of her. The empty place they had set for Joe mysteriously was filled by her. There echoed in him a patience broken, ill-mended in her, the graying hair, the dark stains beneath the eyes, the eyes themselves, haunted, pale, with a kind of loss that he shared with her. When you were small, you were given something to have and hold, and when you were grown it was taken back. Your life, was it? He couldn't say. You only knew it was gone from you.

"Mother won't be up," she said. "If you could wait . . . do you think you could?" She was a child who asks a favor. A child who carries a woman inside and waits forever for her to be born.

He heard himself: "Look . . . put something on and we'll go somewhere nearby and eat."

She looked away as if it might be forbidden her. He was suddenly afraid it was, that she wouldn't go and he would leave and it would end. But she said, "Wait here. I have to dress."

He watched her slight, retreating limp, the bower-bird with a broken wing, her robe brushing the golden harp. He heard its whisper in the gloom. The rug they had sat on the night before was still in place. He could detect like shadows the dampness where they two had sat. Insubstantial shadows that took their place with all the rest. The sea in the painting close at hand lashed at him with a senseless rage. The prancing charger had lost a hoof; the knight, one green and marbled eye. He closed his eyes to wait for her.

It had seemed to him that back from Nam he was given a world to throw away. Nothing was worth the trouble to keep. But this was something you didn't apply to a woman who hoarded every scrap making a heap to fill her life . . . to fill her arms when she woke from sleep, if she ever slept.

"You've gone to sleep," he heard her say.

"Not me," he said. "You could get shot for that in Nam."

He opened his eyes and saw that she had dressed for him, done up her hair. It was unlike the dressing up of the night before, in a way that he could not define.

"Do I look better now?" she asked.

"I never answer a question like that."

He drove her to the place she said. They drank coffee. Beyond the glass, the early pigeons preened for them. He ordered an egg; she ate nothing. The shop was stocked with odds and ends. Over the rim of her coffee cup her eyes swept them abstractedly. She had taken him to a curio shop that was into serving early food. At once she appeared to come to life. Still, her face was the face of a child who wanders alone, staring at all the shop displays to keep from knowing that she is lost. At the moment she seemed unaware of him, unaware that he was in step with her, had been in step for half his life. Somewhere beyond was a radio.

"Your work?" she said. "What is it you do?"

A child with a couple who ate at a table next to them was staring at him. "Not anything at the moment," he said. He did not want to speak of it. His past was like the curio shop, crammed with memories of jobs that hadn't worked out for him. "The war never went away," he said. "Was it that way with Joe, you think?"

"He never talked about the war."

"Tell me how he died," he said.

She smiled at him and turned her head.

"Don't tell me if it hurts to say."

"Joseph had my mother's thing. Except with him it was quicker, you know."

"I wish I had kept in touch with him."

"Well, now you have."

"When it's too late."

She seemed uneasy with talk of Joe, frightened perhaps. She folded, unfolded her paper napkin. He brought himself to say it at last: "I wish I could do something fine for you. I have no money. I lost my job."

He felt her answer sweep his face: "There isn't a thing I need," she said.

He watched her pale and restless hands. Today, he saw, they were free of rings. The fact was vaguely moving. "I need to work on a ranch somewhere. Out in the open." He laughed then. "Away from Nam. In the city it gets me by the throat."

Her eyes rested upon his own. "Men can go any place they dream." He heard the faint cry in her voice.

He stood then and was telling her, "I'm trying to see Joe in your face," aware that he hadn't tried before, aware that he hadn't wanted to.

She covered her face and shook her head.

While he paid the bill she lingered over a glass swan molded of various shades of green. When he bought it for her, her eyes filled. "I'm sorry," she said as she brushed the tears. "You shouldn't have spent your money for this. It's sure I'll never see you again."

They had scattered pigeons to reach the car. "I wouldn't be too sure of that."

"Yes," she said, "be sure of it. Somewhere it's written down in stone."

They sat in the early morning damp. She appeared preoccupied, but he felt her as keenly aware of him as she had been on the day before, walking in grass that was full of rain, weaving him into the falling dusk. . . . The scent of her skin was in his mouth, as if he had lain with her all night. She stroked the green swan in her lap. She held it up before her face, and her pale eyes came alive with green. Then with her lips she brushed its throat. With a kind of shock, he felt that she had brushed his own. "I scatter myself into all my things. I'm made of them . . . crystal, shell. . . . That little bird you told about. I try to make a beautiful world. . . ." She broke off and looked away. "But sometimes I'm lost in it. I get lost. . . . I mustn't tell you this," she said.

He was falling headlong into her voice. It rang with the listening, longing note that now at night was a part of him.

"Are you ever lost in a world you made?"

He tried to focus on her words. "I'm lost in one that was made for me."

Her eyes were turned to him with sorrow. He kissed her hand. And suddenly the hand was Joe's drawing him from the rain of fire.

She withdrew her hand and turned away. Her withdrawal was a reminder that she was still in mourning, that all departures after a death repeat the death or echo it. Even his own departure, perhaps. He drove her home through streets that grimly took on the day, through neighborhoods where the houses slept. At the door he asked, "Will your mother let me say goodbye?"

"Yes," she said, "she wants you to."

He stood in the parlor and waited for them. The cord from the fixture overhead hung free of the lamp with the curious shade. He watched it sway in a breath of air. Along the river in Viet Nam the serpents swung from branches and dropped. At dawn he would find them on the deck.

The old lady wheeled herself in to him. She was quite alone. She was wearing some sort of robe, he saw. The wig of the night before was gone, and her sparse gray hair was drawn back tightly from her face, so tightly it gave her a look of pain with her lips pursed to endure the pain. Or pursed with cunning. He could not tell.

"I hope to come back again," he said.

She stared at him with her crafty eyes. Before their dominion he dropped his own. She slowly withdrew from the folds of her robe a photograph, framed, which she held to her breast. "You have likely wondered why it is that we have no pictures of Joseph around. It's just that his loss is fresh to us, and the sight of his face would be too much."

"I understand."

"But this is my favorite, made when you knew him, when he was young. He changed so much in later years. I wanted to share it with you," she said. She held it out with a little smile.

He took it from her. For a long moment he looked at it, while he steeled himself to conceal the shock. He had never seen the face before.

"A good likeness, wouldn't you say?" She was smiling still.

"Yes," he said, "I think it is." He handed the photograph back to her.

Tina was standing by the door.

"I wish I had a copy for you. But this is the only one I have."

"Yes, ma'am," he said, "I understand. Thank you for letting me see it," he said. "I'll get my bag and be on my way."

She nodded and wheeled away from him and through the doorway from which she had come.

He stood in silence. He did not look at Tina's face. She turned and went into the garden. After a moment he followed her. "I'll get my bag."

Without a word she led him back inside the house and down the hall. Outside the door of her room she stopped. "What is it?" she said. "I saw your face." Her voice broke. She was trembling.

He looked away. "It wasn't the Joe I knew in Nam."

She was holding the swan he'd bought for her, and now she pressed it to her face.

"I can't understand," he said to her. "This was the number he gave to me. The same address. I wrote him here. I called him once. Or could it have been that he called me?"

"It doesn't matter."

"It does matter."

"Why?" she said. She was crying now. "It's one of those things. Names and places are crazy things."

"Maybe I never got it from Joe, the telephone number and this address. Maybe it came from the army, and some computer fouled it up and matched a Joe with another's address."

"Don't think about it," she pled with him.

Swiftly he took her in his arms. He felt as if he folded wings. "I think your mother mustn't know."

"No," she said, "she mustn't know."

"I'll write," he said.

"Why?" she asked. "Why would you write?"

Bewildered yet, he stroked her hair, smoothing the dark into the gray, feeling it live beneath his hand. The knowledge of it steadied him and was the single thing he knew. "Because I have failed the two of you. And maybe I have failed Joe."

He released her then and walked to his room. The blinds were drawn against the day. He left them so while he made the bed, with care as if it had once been Joe's. He leaned above it, stroking the sheets, humbled by years that had swept them apart, haunted and homesick for the war, for its crazy fear that had kept them locked inside its hour, sick with longing to *be* with it before it had cast its long spell.

He sat on the bed and willed himself on the boat again. It was morning, with early fog. They were going nowhere into the sun, trailing a shadow dark as night. He was struck with a vision of startled birds flying out of the tall grass as if each blade of it took wing. Memories winged in a shrill release, till the cloud of them threatened to darken his sky. But he held Joe cornered inside his brain. He always had. If he let him out, he would let out the cry that Joe saved him for years that would hollow him out . . . saved him for nothing . . . for a woman waiting outside the door, who had nothing, yet everything, to do with them both.

Impossibly, he heard her breath. The sun was restless in the blinds. He thought of the fireflies in her room, pricking the dusk of it with light. Her place had been with a memory, the memory of Joe and Nam. Now she belonged with another — the memory of his wife that endless mirrors repeated, like mirrors repeating the room he was shown, until he wanted to smash them.

He picked up his bag. He opened the door and she was there.

She drew him back inside the room. "Kiss me goodbye. She mustn't see."

He took her in his arms again and kissed her slowly, knowing her lostness one with his.

She broke from him. She walked away with her broken wing and turned to him. Her voice was stone. "You see my limp. It's what she has. We'll need someone. She says we will . . . later, we will. You see how practical we are. I have no brother. I have no father. I have no lover. I have this. And I have your friend."

He waited for her.

"We rent this house where he used to live, and it's come to be . . . it's like we rent his name as well. I guess you could say we rent this man, whoever he is, to belong to us. We rent his blood to be in our veins. The calls come. And we say he's dead instead of moved. Do you hear me what I'm trying to say? People who move are like the dead. They never come back. It's like they went away to war, the way he did, and never came back."

She walked to the window. She touched the blinds and splintered the light. "When the phone rings, he becomes her son. He turns into a brother for me. It's almost like a play, you see. It's like a play that turned to real. At first I used to dream of him . . . how we played together when we were small, how he cared for me, took care of me. I never let my mother know I was dreaming this . . . this crazy thing. Sometimes I open the door of my room. He is playing there among my things. He is still a child and he runs and hides. And then I think it belonged to him, this room of mine, when he was young, too young for war, and its beautiful things are there for him. I grew to love him more than I loved the brother I had who died so young. It's true . . . I had a brother who died."

He heard her words like distant guns across a lake, not close enough to be meant for him.

She limped to him from across the room. "His friends come. I would die with joy to have such friends. I would go to war if it got me friends. This Joe of yours, when the phone rings, we make him die all over again."

In a kind of anger she brushed her tears. "I only cry when it's in the play. This isn't the play. This is me saying to you the things we do. . . . One of them wanted to marry me. He gave the room so many things. He promised me a child some day. But he went away. . . . One day from halfway round the world he sent me a bird of green jade. It's real jade, I'm sure it is." She turned to him with imploring eyes. "If he bothered to send it from so far, and if he had wanted to marry me, wouldn't you say it was really jade?"

"Yes," he said.

"I treasure it as jade," she said. She circled the room with her pale eyes. "I treasure the bird you bought for me."

He dismissed it with a laugh.

"You gave it to me. I'm given a thing, it makes me born all over again. The jade . . . the jade I never deserved. It was got with a lie. And so was yours." She covered her face with both her hands.

"No," he said, taking down her hands. "I bought it because it belonged with you. I don't think of Joe when I'm with you." I think of my wife instead, he thought. The knowledge filled him with rage and pain.

She turned away. "My mother says it's what we must do. She's so hard . . . so very hard. You noticed it? How hard she is? At times she's in terrible pain, she says, but I don't believe it when she does. She says it to make me so afraid I'll tell the lie I'm supposed to tell. And when I tell it I try to think of my little brother, who *is* dead. Sometimes I hardly mind the lie. Sometimes it could break my heart in two. I mind with you. I mind with you."

"How long?" he asked. "How long a lie?"

She shook her head from side to side. "Since we came and the calls began. A long lie. Six years of it."

He did not ask how many there were. How many friends, how many lies, and which she had minded least and most; and each a betrayal of himself and a brief moment when they had kissed. "You loved him, the man who sent the jade?"

"I almost did. I loved him enough. He was very kind. . . . I want to ask you something," she said. "Would it make any difference in loving me if I was the sister of Joseph or not?"

He closed his eyes to think of it. He saw the deck of the boat in Nam and falling down in Cap's blood and Joe's hand slipping from him, grabbing his wrist to get a hold. "It wouldn't make any difference," he said, but he didn't know if it would or not. There was a single thing he knew, and a single thing he had to ask: "She could have let me walk away. Why did she show me the photograph?"

"That was my father when he was young. She brings it out to make an end."

"Because I'm a loser, you might say?"

Her eyes filled. "Because I am. Because some day I must have someone. You would make me happy, I can tell. The way you are . . . the way you are. You make a place for a woman to be. That bird that makes a place and waits. I wait to be the one to come. She says I mustn't look for that. But I do look. I have to look." With both her hands she drew down his face to dash her mouth against his own. He felt her tears. "But this way . . . it's a way for us to find someone. And if it isn't going to work, she wants an end to it, she says."

"She wants the room for someone else. Well, she has it back. She has you back." His anger caught her and crushed her face against his breast. Her hair was spilling over his hand. It was like turning in his dream to hold his wife and she was there. To wake and she was really there. . . . He gave her back and watched her leave, with her broken wing, her tumbled hair and the sun fingering its gray.

At the door she turned. Her voice shrilled and broke for him. "I'm not her daughter. Her sister," she said.

In total silence he took it in.

"And so I'm older than you think. The other ones I never told. I tell you because . . . it's the only thing I have to give."

He gave her the only words he had. "I never think about old," he said. "Since Nam I only think of it: you make it through or else you don't, and maybe it doesn't matter which."

"I'm trying to make it through," she said.

Then she let in the morning sun and the distant cry the traffic made and left him at the mercy of them. His words were lost in the traffic's cry: "So you let her make a lie of you."

But in his arms she was not a lie.

He picked up his bag and left the house. He did not want the phone to ring, to hear her voice: "I'm sorry to tell you my brother is dead. . . ." But surely it would be months, years, till another voice would ask for Joe. Perhaps his own was the final one.

Down the road a ways it came to him that the Joe he knew was alive somewhere.

The Second Shepherd

WELL BEFORE CHRISTMAS they planned their strategy, how in fact they were going to outwit the season, resolved, as they were, not to have a repeat of the year before when the fateful Day had lumbered toward them. Picking up speed, it had made a rush, and in the end they were flattened out like cartoon characters by a tank. Flat as the crust for a seasonal pie. For in advance they could joke a bit, but they knew that as the Day approached. . . .

Emily came up with the plan in October, and Dan went along. Neither thought it a brilliant course but admittedly better than nothing at all. And then it began to mellow for them. They saw it as almost a given thing, given by little Debbie herself.

They would go to a local orphanage; whoever happened to be in charge would hear them out: You see, they would say, our daughter Debbie, our only child, was taken over a year ago. She was only three. Well, we won't go into the Christmas after. . . . It occurred to us that it would be good to find a child, one of your own, say five years old, and a boy . . . a girl would be too much . . . a girl would really be too much. We'd like to take this boy for the day. Make it a Christmas he'll never forget. Dinner, presents, that sort of thing.

And indeed they were saying these very words, now that it was December first.

It was not the classiest orphanage. It looked as if it could do with help. Perhaps it was why they had picked it out. In front was a brave little turnaround, freshly graveled but spottily bordered with junipers gone patchy brown, in the center a moldering monument scarcely worth a second glance. The lawn was scraps of desperate grass, its spirit quenched. Against the building of yellow brick, hickories slept and dropped their leaves.

Inside, there was a hint of bustle. Down corridors they caught a hum. Through a door ajar they spied a desk, and on the desk was a metal plate. The plate proclaimed "Miss Parmlee." Behind the plate, scarcely clearing it, Miss Parmlee prepared to hear them out.

She was very small, like an orphan child gone to seed. Or like an elf, it occurred to them, as if she had popped from a hole in the ground or out of the woods now winter-brown. She was dressed in brown, her hair was brown. Even her face had faint, brown spots like the junipers in the turnaround. Her leaf-brown eyes looked very wise, not old but wise. And on the alert, as if she could tell what was going on in every single part of the Home. As if you couldn't possibly say something she hadn't heard before.

She listened with the tiniest smile, as if their plan was the usual thing. "Our patrons," she said, "have done so much."

They were surprised and a bit alarmed that a single day with a single child could be construed as patronage. But then they supposed in a way it was, given the need that seemed to prevail and the magnitude of the day proposed. Dan hastened to say, "We don't know what the future holds. We simply wanted to give a Christmas to a child. A boy," he thought to reinforce.

"Put stars in his eyes," Emily thought to add.

Miss Parmlee wrought a professional smile and a personal one at the same time. She was very good with a compound smile. "I understand. A lovely thought, and certainly it can be arranged. If you'll leave the arrangement of it to us. . . . I suppose you wouldn't want to choose." Her tone was a little threatening.

"Oh, no," said Emily. "Whatever you think. The one you think has the greatest need. The boy, that is."

Miss Parmlee's eyes were full of boys. She seemed to be searching for just the one, pulling one in by the tail of his shirt and rejecting him with her other hand. She swiveled her chair away from the desk, and then they saw her emerald socks that bloomed from shoes that yawned unlaced. Jogging shoes, not elfin wear. Indeed the joggers held their gaze.

She caught the gaze and tossed it back. "The halls are tile. Ten years of it and the arches fall. Like bowling pins."

They hastened to avert their eyes. And Emily said, "If I could have the size in advance. For clothes, you know. And what his greatest need would be."

Miss Parmlee said, "You'll be informed."

Afterwards at home they said, "We did the right thing, don't you think?" In bed they clung together and wept. They had not wept for many a night. Will it make it worse? they wanted to know. But no, they said, it's the thing to do. In the tree whose bare limbs brushed their screen they could hear the wind that moaned for them. Around their bed was an empty house. It was very strange that a tiny child could have filled a house, that without her in a bed nearby, the house was void and echoing. Abandoned was perhaps the word, as if a regiment, billeted there, had got their orders and marched at dawn.

They fell into a well of dreams. Their sleeping minds were tossing her, making her laugh, consoling her, pulling her in the red wagon. "Hold on," they cried. Between them she rode the carousel. "Hold on," they said. They watched her holding the horse's mane, rising as they sank from her; then as they rose she was falling away, falling from them till she disappeared. Down . . . down . . . until they woke. That too was strange: that they could dream a single dream.

At times Emily thought that she dragged the wagon through the days, and on it was heaped her memories and tears.

In a week someone called in a breathless voice and gave the size. "Miss Parmlee thinks a coat would be nice."

Later, Emily remarked to Dan: "If they know the size they have the child. If they have the child they have the name. If they have the name, then why can't we?"

"That's logical, of course," he said. "There's really no logic in any of this."

She grew alarmed. "Does that mean you think we've made a mistake?"

"Not a mistake, just not logical."

"I thought," she said, "that's what this was. A very rational, logical move."

He looked the least bit annoyed with her. "Losing a child isn't logical. You just don't cope with it logically."

"So you see this as some crazy . . . scheme." He didn't reply. "Is it crazy to want to help a child?

"It's not," he said. "It's the thing to do."

Reassured, she bought the coat. She took a long time in choosing it. She enlisted his help, of course, with the toys. Confused, bemused, they wandered evenings in toy departments. Their helpless eyes besought the clerks'. Discreetly they spied upon little boys, the ones, to be sure, who had strayed from mothers, and made a note of what they fingered, what they had to be torn from, screaming. Children, they saw, were shoplifters at heart. Some of them got away with it.

They placed themselves in the path of a child. "How old are you, little boy?" said Dan. The little boy rolled his marble eyes, then held up a hand with his fingers outstretched. They trailed him as he hiccuped his way down the narrow aisles. What he lingered before they jotted down. What he touched they bought. They were pleased with their devious ways.

They drove to a hardware store or two to find a bicycle just the size. It came complete with training wheels. The aging clerk with watery eyes explained the use of the training wheels. "They didn't have them in my day." He honked his nose and reassured them, "Allergy. Can't take the sizing in pup tents. You think you might have an interest in one?"

They studied their list and shook their heads.

"Right," he said. "A kid's got to have real vision, you know, to want a tent the middle of winter." He tipped the bike and spun the wheels. "Of course in my day, maybe in yours, a kid didn't try to ride a bike until he was old enough for one. You cracked your skull a couple of times until you got the hang of it. They're pushing them now for kids of three. The way I'm pushing the pup tents. How old is yours?"

"Five," they said, convinced he could sense their subterfuge.

"It's like I say. They're pushing them." He patted the bike. Its seat was covered with tiger skin. "Don't tell your kid the skin is fake. They like to think it's the real thing. Unless you're into conservation. Animals and all that. Some kids now is raised that way." He gave his nose a fearsome honk, rather like an elk, they thought.

They shook their heads.

"Right," he said. "It's against their nature. I give my grandson a BB gun. Anything that moves he shoots. Caterpillars . . . tadpoles."

They paid his price. He honked them to and out the door.

"Why isn't he selling horns?" said Dan.

"That wasn't on our list," she said.

In a grim way they were having fun.

DECEMBER STRUCK. The hour struck. It found them buttressed with heaps of toys and a tree that sparkled with silver and gold. Still they were struck with a vague alarm. They had banked their grief with some hard-won ash, and they shrank from seeing the embers glow. But of course the die was thoroughly cast. When the dinner was cooking away in the stove, or laid to ice, whatever it took, they discussed at length whether Dan should go or whether together they should go. They decided to show a united front.

Once in the car, they were stirred with determined anticipation. "Make someone happy," they assured themselves for the twentieth time. "If we can't be, well, somebody can." And their hearts added that if they could make him happy enough, he would drop some crumbs of it for them.

The Home had bowed the season in with a wreath hung over the monument and the junipers laced with cords of lights. Tinsel winked in the trees for them. Perhaps at night their glory shone.

Miss Parmlee was not in her former haunt. They searched and found her down the hall. She had mounted a chair in a large room and was throwing popcorn, strings of it, across a somewhat needy tree. There were stars cut out of construction paper pinned about where the growth was sparse. To their eyes the tree lacked symmetry. They were torn between vanity and remorse that theirs was done and handsomer far than hers would be. They noted once more her emerald socks. Her joggers lay shuffled off below.

She smiled upon them from her height, as if they had been there all along. "Miss Ellis went off without telling us where she hides the colored balls this year. She calls it something else, I think. I like to call a spade a spade. When it's not around where it should be, it's filched or hidden, take your pick. . . . We'll add them tomorrow when she comes."

It sounded exceedingly strange to them. The tree not done till Christmas was done. But they nodded at her. "Remember us? We're here for the boy."

"Of course you are." She hopped from the tree like a little brown bird, both feet at once. Again, they found her like an elf, one who lived in this very tree. Since the child's death, as the Day approached they thought as well as dreamed as one. "Of course you are." Miss Parmlee stared at the topmost branch.

"Moths have been into the angel again. Miss Ellis has forgotten to spray. And of course she hides the stuff from us." She turned to them. "He's ready for you. Had his bath. We've managed to keep him reasonably clean. Miss Kimbrough has been in charge of that."

"We were never told his name," said Emily.

Miss Parmlee calmly straightened a star. "An oversight. We abound in them. The angel is a case in point. The better part of a wing is gone. Eaten. Devoured. . . . It's Buster," she said. "Not the angel, the child," she explained. "The angel, as I recall, is Herald . . . for 'Hark, the herald angels sing.'" She went into a quiver of mirth.

Emily smiled. "But his real name?"

"It's all he has," Miss Parmlee said. "He was left with the name attached to him. Last year we gave him a choice of them, but he liked 'Buster.' He was used to it."

"I like it too," said Dan at once.

Miss Parmlee gurgled, "What's in a name?" She waved an arm and an emerald foot. "It does have a certain ring," she said. She seemed to them of exceptional cheer. "With 'Buster' doors will open to him that won't for 'Tom,' 'Dick,' or 'Harry,' you know.

With 'Buster' he can raise some . . ." She paused and smiled. "Some Cain," she said.

Her official air was quite dissolved in a seasonal spirit. Or was it spirits? Something Miss Ellis forgot to hide? They almost caught a fragrant hint. Or was it the baking down the hall?

Miss Parmlee tripped to the open door. "Miss Kimbrough, we're ready," she sweetly called. She turned to them. "I'm afraid," she said, "that he has a lisp." She added with a toss of her head, "There's no such thing as a perfect child."

Dan assured her warmly, "We couldn't care less."

"He isn't a very verbal child. You'll hardly notice it, I'm sure."

Quite suddenly he was in their midst. He seemed to have been propelled to them by an unseen agent from the hall. For the head came first, the torso next, and the running feet were abruptly braked. They could only stare. They were looking down at a bearded child. Sandy hair, freckles gone into a winter fade, and a generous, curling, chestnut beard.

Miss Parmlee fairly whooped it out: "Miss Ellis has done it again, I fear. I hope it won't be a problem for you. There really is a child inside. Yesterday was pageant day. She fixed the beards before she left — she likes a Christmas with family, you know — and forgot to say where she hides the stuff that takes them off. Miss Kimbrough has soaked him down to the bone, till his fingers turned to prunes, she said. She thought of giving him a shave. But we'll need the beard again next year. I'm afraid it's there till Miss Ellis comes." Miss Parmlee smoothed an errant curl of the chestnut beard. "Miss Ellis is the hub of the wheel. When she's off for the day she hides the hub."

They found themselves at a loss for words. The greetings they had prepared for him were suddenly not the thing at all. The toys they had bought were not the thing. Their very selves were not the thing. He seemed not a child but a wise old man cut down to size . . . to the five-year size they had specified.

"Of course he loves it," Miss Parmlee said. "He'd like to wear it the rest of his life, at least until he grows his own."

They stared at him. He skimmed them with blue, retreating eyes.

"He's the Second Shepherd," she thought to add. "He carried a crook and I think a lamb. Buster, did you carry a lamb?"

He stared at the floor till she snapped two fingers. "Yeth, ma'am."

"You see," she said, but whether she meant the lisp or lamb was hard to tell.

She introduced them all around. And then they drove away with him. They had planned to travel with him between the two of them, but the beard seemed to require space. They opened the back and in he slipped. Driving down the street, they could almost believe he wasn't there.

When they arrived they girded their loins and summoned their cheer. He sat quite still in the corner of the car, looking solemn and disengaged. He had to be urged to descend to them and partake of the joys they had prepared.

They hustled him down and up the steps and into the house where the tree shone. He lowered his head to look at it from under his brows. His eyes slid over the mound of gifts, over the bicycle parked near by and the yellow truck, over the trumpet hung from a branch, the set of drums just under it, the bat nudging the mitt above . . . over the ball and the Car City, the Farm Set with cows and lambs and chickens on spindly yellow legs, and the wagon, red with streaks of gold, the tractor big enough to ride, and half a dozen G.I. Joes surrounding a Space Vehicle Launch Complex. Its operation defeated them, but they thought, with his help, they could make it work. The fireman's suit was on a chair, and the coat, the carefully chosen coat, was boxed up with a red bow.

They urged him heartily to approach. He hung back. "It's yours," they said. "It's all yours."

Slowly he approached the tree. He would not touch. He simply looked. Detached or stunned? They could not tell. Whatever he felt was lost to them in the lush rain forest of his beard. His eyes were clearly visible, centuries old and a little sad.

They looked at each other in dismay, at their gold and frankincense and myrrh, all certified irresistible. Amazement drowned their deep-down grief. Together they became the child who waits upon parental pleasure to reveal where he has gone astray.

He took three steps to the bike erect on its training wheels. He soberly gazed at the tiger skin seat.

"Would you like to try it out?" said Dan.

The boy sighed and shook his head but did not draw his eyes away.

"It really is for you," said Dan.

The boy sighed and went on gazing.

Emily opened the red box with the bow and held up the coat for him to see. She slid it on him, first one sleeve and then the other. He did not resist. While she was stooping to button it, he gazed across her at the tree. She found she could not bring herself to invade the privacy of his beard, which covered the buttons at the top. "It fits!" she exclaimed. "And it looks so good. It looks fine." She appealed to Dan. "Isn't it just a perfect fit?"

"It is," said Dan, "and it looks warm. It really does look very warm."

The boy stood as still as the tree. His eyes swept the two of them. They felt a heaviness of his heart like a chill of the early fog that dawn dispels.

"Do you like it, Buster? Please like it just a little," she coaxed. Deep in thought, he inclined his head.

"Good," she said and took it off. "I hope you won't grow up too fast."

Soberly he perused the gifts, but he made no move to approach them. Perhaps it was the cut of his beard. There are wise beards and foolish beards. The cut of his was very wise. He seemed too wise for foolish joy.

"The tractor you can ride," said Dan.

The boy fastened his eyes on it.

Dan beckoned her into the kitchen. "I think we should leave him alone with it. He's shy with it while we're around."

She stood at the sink. "What is wrong?" Sadness threatened to flood her heart. The slightest thing that went amiss would find its way, like a river the sea, to the old sorrow that lay in her. "Maybe he's hungry is what it is. Maybe I should dish it up."

Dan reached for a lighter note. "I didn't envision Christmas dinner with Buster the bearded wise child."

"Not a wise man, a shepherd," she said.

"Of course he was miscast." Dan sighed. "I can't seem to get past the beard. From the look of it, he's more a man of the world than I. Do you think there's a kid inside the hair?"

Tears stung her throat. She swallowed them. "I'm not sure. But we should eat."

He agreed at once. "Food is the greatest leveler. It puts men on an equal plane. Even a wise man has to eat."

"A shepherd," she reminded him.

But first they had to look in on him. He had backed away from the laden tree and was gravely positioned against a chair. He had not bothered to climb and sit. Perhaps he felt it was not allowed.

Dan, swooping him up and into the chair, was surprised to find how light he was. He had not touched a child since his own. For a moment he seemed to have lifted her.

They sat in silence across from him. His head had sunk. He seemed to commune with his jungle beard. Emily felt as if the Christmases past and those to come had all been piled in the red wagon for her to drag the rest of her days.

Dan asked in a conversational tone, "What made you want to be a shepherd?"

Buster raised his head. He gazed at them. His freckles were like the shadows of leaves, the brown leaf spots in Miss Parmlee's face. "You got to be chothe," they heard him say. The words were muffled a bit with hair.

They were actually stunned to hear him speak.

"By God?" Emily asked in her softest voice.

He gave his head an impatient shake. "Mith Ellith," he said.

"Of course," she smiled.

His eyes were solemn. "Mary got chothe by Him, but Thally was chothe by her." They tried in vain to decipher it. He scanned their faces. He sucked in his breath. "Mary was Jethuth mother."

"Sally?"

"The'th a girl."

"She possibly played the part," said Dan.

"Did you come?" Buster asked. They seemed to have found the magic key to unlock his speech.

"To the pageant? I'm afraid we didn't know."

"Lotth of people did."

"I'm sure it was lovely."

"Thally dropped her gum on Baby Jethuth."

In the midst of his general sadness there appeared a little flash of amusement tempered, albeit, with disapproval; but it lapsed into a somber detachment. They found his gaze upon the tree.

They saw it lifted to scan the star and slowly glide to the things beneath. They saw it fasten upon the bike. They felt it mount the tiger seat and sit in bearded contemplation.

Dan gave the key another turn. "Would you like to tell us about the pageant?"

The boy was still. He shook his head. His word-hoard, once unlocked for them, had proved to be a paltry one. Or else a burden damped it down. Mourning seemed to wrap him round. Silence fell upon the room. It was hard to believe they had heard his voice. Even the tree stopped sparkling.

Emily felt herself reduced to dust, swept back into another season. "God!" she said, as if the boy weren't there at all. "What's wrong with us?"

Dan heard the panic in her throat. He took her hand.

"It's just that he might help us out! We've tried so hard."

"Shall I put a record on?" he whispered.

She shook her head. "Please, not that." Music, she knew, would make her break.

"I think we all need food," he said.

She fled to the kitchen to dish it up. He helped her get it on the table laid with a holly-imprinted cloth and centered with a ring of angels, tiny golden cheeks near bursting, puffing into golden horns.

They pinned their hopes to the power of food. Each item of it time had approved, endorsed it potent to lift the heart, rejoice the senses, every one. Cranberries burst, spilling red, fragrant, thick, their wild and bitter tamed to sweet. Hadn't they graced the Pilgrims' feast? The golden turkey ran with juice. Dan carved it with a festive air. They beamed upon the shepherd child. They became his flock. They followed him. Darkness hovered about their souls. They asked that he lead them to the fold. And thus it was they heaped his plate, wooing his favor, his mercy, even, and yes, to strengthen him for his task.

He sat and looked at his plate in awe. Tears came trickling down his beard to fall into his mashed potatoes.

They stared and then laid down their forks.

"What is it? Tell us," they pled with him.

He sucked in his breath and raked a fist across his eyes.

Dan said, "This isn't working well." He looked at Emily, who began to cry. He stood up then. "I can't be expected to take this."

He took Buster firmly by the hand and led him into the living room and placed him on top of the fireman's suit. Emily sat down before the child. Dan left them crying. He walked away and out the back as if he might never be coming back. She heard the door. She heard the latch. And then her heart began to break. They had thought and dreamed and grieved as one, and now he had left her to grieve alone.

He returned to find them still in tears and sat down beside his wife. Emily looked at him with clouded eyes. "It's made it worse. . . ." She could not go on.

He put his arm around her then. "I feel the same" was all he said.

"So what did we do wrong?" she asked.

He stared at Buster. He said in a voice that was carefully calm: "What is it you don't like here?"

Tears were glistening in the beard. The boy sighed deeply and sighed again. He tried to speak and tried again. "How could you guyth do thith to me?"

They were stung and stunned. "Do what?" they said.

But he shook his head and turned from them.

Emily rose and knelt to him. "What?" she asked. His sorrow threatened to engulf her too. But gently she patted his wet hand. "Please say," she whispered. "I had a little girl one time. I could understand."

He gazed with sorrow into her eyes. "They got a party," he whispered back.

When she kissed him on the neck, she felt his beard upon her cheek. She returned to Dan.

"What is it?" he said.

"They're having a party back at the Home. We've taken him away from his friends."

"Nobody ever told us," he said.

"We never asked. We were thinking only about ourselves . . . and that was why we never asked."

He stared at her and nodded slowly. He stood and twice he circled the room. He grew indignant and then resigned. "Well, hadn't we better get him back? Before it's over. Unless, of course, it already is."

Grimly then he gathered the toys and made three trips to the car with them, while Buster watched with reddened eyes.

She got the white cake from the kitchen. She held it on its crystal throne. "They might want it," she explained to him. Or to herself. "It's very good. It's my recipe for birthday cake. Of course I left the candles off." She could not think what to do with it. "I had such a good time icing it." She sat down with the cake in her lap. "You see," she said, her eyes on the cake, "we were thinking you would want to come. We should have asked you first, I know. . . ." She did not go on.

His eyes were full of a pain they shared, a pain that the day had magnified. She asked the wise man who sat with her: "Why is Christmas so very sad?" She could hear Dan slam the trunk of the car. She wanted the wisdom of a child while still there was time. . . . while they were alone. "Do you know why it is?"

He shook his head. He was only a shepherd after all.

"Was it happy for you the last time?"

He closed his eyes on a memory. He nodded slowly.

She told him then, "Last time for me was very sad. My little girl was gone . . . just gone. But the time before was the very best I ever had. And what I think we were doing with you . . . I couldn't bear a little girl . . . we were mixing up the best and the worst and making a Christmas in between the best one and the worst one . . . and then forgetting to ask you if you wanted to help . . . to come," she said. "Will you be happier if we take you back?"

He nodded at once, his eyes like moons upon her face.

"I'm glad," she said. "I'm very glad." She got a napkin and dried his beard.

They left the table with all its promise. They put him again in the back of the car, perched this time on his mountain of gifts. The bicycle was stashed in the trunk. The Home, when they neared, had a crestfallen air. The tinseled trees, the wreath on the door, all looked as if there had been a rain. Inside, it was another thing. The smell of a living sweetness (cake?), and down the hall the voice of the sea, a billowing of liquid sound, and riding it, like the crest of a wave that was shoreward bound, a call they knew as Miss Parmlee's came. From out of the deep it beckoned them.

Buster had raced ahead of them. They could but follow. Into the big room he shrieked his arrival, and all the children flocked around. Instantly he and a bearded child fell to pummeling one another, grappling, yelling, rubbing beards, till in a ferocious clinch they fell. Arms, legs, and beards were intertwined. They rolled in a paroxysm of joy.

At Emily's side Miss Parmlee stood in a pink dress with billowing sleeves and holly in her troubled hair. "The two shepherds," she whooped at them. "Miss Ellis let them be the shepherds so both of them could have a beard. Regular Siamese twins, you know. That's why they're attacking one another. Bosom friends. Inseparable."

The room was filled with a din of children. Hands were filled with paper cups and cupcakes pierced with candles aflame, and all the flames in constant motion seemed a part of the general din.

Beyond was a table decked with holly, and in the center a bowl of punch all cherry red. On a single tray there were cupcakes with flames that fluttered with children's breath that came from mouths that were cherry red.

Miss Parmlee was saying, "We have to watch them closely now. They love the candles best of all, but Jimmy, the other shepherd, I regret to say has singed his beard. The rest of the year we're very strict. No matches allowed, all by the book. Children are drawn to fire, you know. Something primitive, I suppose. It's never wise to stifle the craving. They grow up arsonists, you know. So once a year we give them fire. So far, we've had no catastrophes. A singed eyebrow or two . . . and the beard."

She executed a little shuffle. Beneath her skirt, which reached her heels, they caught a glimpse of her emerald socks. They saw that her air of elfin queen had been replaced by a lilting, even a carnival, air. She had clearly been into the bowl of punch. Her mouth was rimmed with the cherry red. She seemed to have been into something else. Whatever had livened the morning for her was livening more her afternoon.

"All year we quench the flame within . . ." She struck her breast with a fist concealed in billowing sleeve. "I'm fond of a little flame myself." She produced a slender cannister. "I carry this in case," she said. "And all my staff has like provision."

"Tell us what it is," said Emily.

Miss Parmlee smiled with condescension. "It's for fires, what else?" she said, and she treated them to a modest squirt.

Dan said, "I'll get the things from the car."

Miss Parmlee followed him with her eyes. She placed a hand on Emily's arm. "Let me send you refreshments now. There's a chair behind you. Feel at home."

She wove her way through the children, skillfully keeping her sleeves afloat yet safe from flame. Emily felt she had done it for endless seasons, dodging flames in the same dress. Not once had the sleeves been caught by them. But then she was nimble in emerald socks. And of course she carried her cannister. She sang above the children's clamor: "Blow out your candle, little ones, before you begin to eat your cake."

A small boy, loath to lose his fire, was holding his little cake aloft and nibbling into it from the bottom.

Dan was in and out of the door, making a pile of gifts in the corner. He fetched the bicycle from the trunk. From nowhere Buster was on the pile. He clapped the fireman's hat to his head. He swung himself to the tiger skin seat and raced his bike around the room. The children followed, then fell back. The clamor ceased. They watched in awe.

Dan came and stood with Emily. "Our little shepherd is out of control. I guess he likes it after all."

But the little shepherd slowed his speed and pedaled to where Miss Parmlee stood beside the tree as she reached to adjust a popcorn string. Dismounting with a princely air, he laid his hat on the tiger seat. Abruptly he abandoned both. They saw him downing a cup of punch, and then he was downing the other shepherd, rolling over and under the table.

Miss Parmlee billowed across to them. "The problem," she said, "is the other children. They won't have theirs until tomorrow. That's why we give them fire today."

They could but stare.

"We have an excellent arrangement here. The toy store gives us everything half price tomorrow. Slash, slash . . ." She flagged the air. "Miss Ellis will be back by then and drive the van into town for it. A splendid arrangement, don't you think?"

"But today . . . ," said Dan.

"Precisely," she said. "I wonder if you would help me carry these generous gifts to a room in back. Buster wants them put away till the other children get their own. A laudable impulse, wouldn't you say? We never let one die on the vine."

"We're sorry," said Emily. "We didn't know."

Miss Parmlee brushed the breach aside. "We have our quaint little customs here."

"I guess we've blown it again," said Dan. "We separate two Siamese shepherds, and now it seems we're out of sync . . ."

"What's in a day?" Miss Parmlee said, as she had inquired, "What's in a name?" only a matter of hours ago. "If a child is born at midnight, who's to say what day is which?"

"Was He?" said Emily, wondering.

"Who's to say He wasn't?" Miss Parmlee said. "My staff has voted and taken a stand."

On what? they thought. Their spirits had grown too faint to care. Dan waded in to retrieve the bike. Emily felt at sea in a leaky boat. She saw Miss Ellis cast her vote and hide it in her jogging shoe.

Miss Parmlee turned and then turned back. "Sit down," she said to Emily briskly, quite as if to an errant orphan. "That way you can eat your muffin in comfort. Don't mind the crumbs. Crumbs on the floor is what today is all about."

Emily sat and closed her eyes. I want this day to be wiped away. I don't want any crumbs of it. With her eyes shut she recalled that she had brought a cake. It was in the car on the front seat. She knew that she would leave it there. It would certainly be the wrong kind or the wrong day.

Although it was still on the front seat, curiously she could smell the cake. She opened her eyes. Beside her was a little girl, brown of hair and red of mouth, with a smudge of icing on her cheek. She held out a muffin with a lighted candle.

"That is Sally," Miss Parmlee said, sailing by with a load of Buster's gifts, leading the way for Dan to follow, calling back, "Send her back for a cup of punch."

Dan leaned and whispered, "It's Thally. Remember?"

Emily, shocked into automation to find a little girl so close, took the muffin from the child. The top of it was frosted white. The small red candle made it glow. In her hand the child clutched a similar muffin. She held it out. "Hold mine," she said in a clear voice.

Emily held them both, her heart in her mouth, while the child ran away and then returned, pushing in front of her a chair. She pushed it up to face Emily's chair, until the two chairs almost touched. Then she climbed to sit. Her knees brushed Emily's. She smiled as she held both hands for her cake.

Emily gave it back. *I must leave at once.* In vain her eyes sought Buster out, as if his presence could save her now. She had followed the shepherd to the cliff and now he had abandoned her. Unreasonably she felt betrayed. She saw how far it was to fall . . . *I told them not a little girl.*

Sally gazed at her over the candlelight. She said at last in a solemn voice, so close that her breath stirred Emily's flame, "Baby Jesus was my own little baby. He got bigger and died. Did you know that?"

Emily nodded through her tears.

The children's voices sank to whispers. The candles bobbed like fireflies in a room grown dim as if with dusk. She seemed to have been waiting days . . . even years in this twilit room, waiting to heal or else to break. She sat in the shadow of this child and the child in hers. *This little one doesn't deserve my dark. She doesn't deserve the dark in me.*

She grew aware that the girl was wearing her pageant dress. She must have begged to be allowed. It was pale blue and covered her shoes; its hood had fallen to cradle her throat.

Emily tried to look away. But the little girl was so very near and her face and robe had filled the room, until this child was the Mary mother who bore a child she would live to lose . . . and at once the child who would be lost . . . who had been lost. This is my child and I am she, this little mother to lose her own. A tiny robe could enfold them both. For by the robe the child and the mother were rendered one.

For a moment Emily was overwhelmed. She felt herself summed up, proclaimed, her grief mirrored and understood. She heard its echo in the child. She heard it spoken and blessed in her. She sat and held her breath to hear. She knew the voices in the room, grown separate, distinct, and each for her. The heavy wagon of memories she had been dragging through her days. She felt the memories changing shape, begin to settle, make room for more, make room for every living thing. Her candle made her a little hearth. At length its warmth had reached her heart. At length her tears began to dry.

The little girl, who was smiling now, made her candle dip in a joyous dance. Even after it had guttered out, spilling its wax all over the cake, the flame of it was in her eyes.

Niagara Falls

W HEN THE STORES put up their Christmas tinsel and piped
their jingles into the street, Tessa bought three darling gifts and
wrapped them for herself. Then she put them away somewhere.
When she opened them on Christmas Day her memory had gotten so rusty that she could almost be surprised. Not really amazed
but just surprised. They were things she had always wanted, like
a skillet with Silverstone. It was not like depending on relatives,
none of which she had, who ninety-nine times in a hundred would
never hit you right.

But sad to say, her memory was getting so full of holes that once
she forgot where the gifts were hid. It bothered her to know they
were in the house somewhere, like children hiding and watching
her. If she could only forget them, but her memory was not so bad
as that. She sat on the floor beside her tree and said to herself, "You
old fool!" She thought of writing a little note and pinning it to her
will: "If you're nosing around my house and find three packages
Christmas-wrapped, I'd like to have them buried with me. Un-
opened, please, if you don't mind."

When Mabel Chum announced she was moving into a home, a private home for retired ladies, Tessa asked what kind of home.

"Well, widows who can't be bothered with things."

"What things?"

"All things. Remembering them."

"You mean they can't remember things?"

"Well, more than likely they could, you know, but they're tired of the strain of it."

"Yes," said Tessa, "it is a strain."

"And doing things is an awful strain."

"Yes," said Tessa, "it is a strain. Christmas is a particular strain."

So Mabel Chum explained it all. The Teasdale sisters, Doll Baby and Baby Doll, so close in age they were almost twins, had both on the very same day in June expressed themselves as thoroughly sick of remembering. That day in June when Baby Doll stepped into a tub and nothing emerged from the faucet except the sound of a crude person winding up to spit. They were sick of remembering the water bill. Remembering every bloody thing told on them in every way. At times they got their dentures switched.

A retirement home was damned expensive, Mabel said, and run like a prison for people unlucky enough to be old. "Which we are not," Mabel told her. "No way are we the aged." So the Teasdale sisters, who owned the house that had been in their family a number of years (they couldn't be bothered with adding them up), came up with the notion of renting space to other simpatico ladies. Much cheaper than a retirement home and, God, more flexibility. The rent could be pooled to send out for meals, to hire a woman to come and clean and a handy man to keep the yard and do a number of handy things. Someone good we can trust, they said, trust to remember the things we can't, that is, the things we prefer to forget. One of the ladies must come with a written guarantee that she could remember to add and subtract and write all checks to pay the bills.

After a very discreet interview, the vote fell to one named Bessie Fortescue, not the most amiable lady, but she could remember her fractions, she said. And in a display of arrogance she recited the times tables up through five. She vowed she recalled the capitals of every state that was worth a hoot, but Baby Doll cried, "Hold, enough!" Her Shakespeare was not entirely gone but lingered on her fringes.

On recommendation of Mabel Chum, Tessa was chosen to make a fourth. "Enough for bridge," said Baby Doll.

But Doll Baby stared her down. "We're sick of remembering what's been played."

"I forgot," said Baby Doll.

Bessie Fortescue demanded another. (She recalled her tables up through five.) An extra rent would pay the bills. And if they wanted a man who was extra handy, she said, well, Bessie recalled her division too. She told them how much the rent would be. She weasled a discount for herself to pay for the strain of arithmetic. The Teasdale sisters were exempt from rent. They owned the house. They paid the damnable taxes.

A discreet inquiry came up with another, a recently widowed Ethel Malone, who found herself a lady of means but couldn't think what to do with them. She declared she could not do a thing. "My husband did everything," she said. "And when I tell you every-thing"— she leaked a little and mopped her eyes —" I mean to tell you everything. He wouldn't let me do a thing! I never had to think."

"Was that a good thing?" asked Mabel Chum.

"I don't know. Since I didn't do, how am I to know?"

Baby Doll said, "There's logic in that."

And Doll Baby inquired, "Have you thought of entering a retirement home?"

But Ethel drew back in horror at that. "All the arrangements, I never could. And all the moving, I never could."

Baby Doll promised, "Join us and we'll get you moved as soon as we find our linchpin." She referred, of course, to the handy man.

The Teasdale sisters phoned in an ad, and after a week of it Greeley knocked. A tall man but not overly tall, with a tanned face and a white moustache — but not too white. The grayish white of a granite stone. Like a modest tombstone for a child, one who had died at birth, they thought. Hands with impressive tendons, arms with impressive sinews, and shoulders that rippled with muscles beneath his checkered shirt. They noted with satisfaction that he owned a pickup truck. Yes, he would certainly do. But they conducted an interview, just to be businesslike. His wife was dead, they uncovered.

"Have you served your country?" asked Baby Doll.

He inclined his head.

"Which war was that?" asked Mabel Chum. She was faking it, they knew. Her wars were down the drain.

He seemed to guess, for he simply smiled.

"An honorable discharge?" Bessie asked.

He inclined his head.

"Were you wounded?" Tessa asked.

He smiled again. Before they knew it, three buttons of his shirt were ripped undone to reveal a gray and feathered chest, and curling through the feathers a sickle moon of a scar, the shape of a scimitar, as if in the making he had tangled with a Turk.

"Hold, enough!" cried Baby Doll.

When the interview was done, Bessie Fortescue sniffed. "He looked like a bloody Crusader to me."

He had been hired on the spot and sent to Ethel Malone.

GREELEY WAS ALL THE NAME HE GAVE, at least all he acknowl-
edged. It was a pleasure to watch him mow. He ripped the grass
like a tiger. It was a joy to watch him dig. He cut the earth like
butter. And when he washed the windows, they squealed like a
hungry pig. It had been a little less of a joy to watch him moving
Ethel Malone, who got in his way and chanted: "I don't know how
to do a thing. My husband did it all."

Tessa heard him mutter, "It may have been what killed him."

Bessie F, as they called her — they couldn't be burdened with
Fortescue — pronounced him a little tacky. Why? they asked her.
Tacky? Why? He sweats like a peasant, she told them. Well what
did she expect of a man who was getting paid to be handy?

"He speaks well," said Tessa. "I think he speaks like a gentleman."

"A gentleman," said Bessie F, "would have another name. Is
Greeley his first or his last name? Or is it a criminal alias? He wants
his checks just Greeley."

There was a little inequity concerning the ladies' cars. The
garage, of course, was the Teasdales'. It housed their Cadillac. The
others must park their cars in the street or anywhere they could
scrounge a spot. Tessa's car was a Buick, one of the lesser models
and one with a little age. It stood beneath a tree. Tessa felt a pres-
sure to keep her car shipshape. In reference to Ethel's car, she had
overheard the "tacky" word from the lips of Bessie F.

So after her trip to the hair salon, she drove her car to a car
wash, a thing she had not done in years. She thought she had never
done it, but then she could not be sure. Afterwards she declared
it the worst event of her life. She had forgotten to roll it up, the
window at her side. The hairdo she had paid for was swiftly flot-
sam and jetsam. And when she got the window up she sat in sheer
dismay, while the rain fell and the soap fell and the brushes came
from everywhere to wash her sins away. Under a massive deluge,
naked to the wrath of God, she was shooting over Niagara Falls

crammed in a leaky bucket. There was no other way to describe it. She pronounced herself assaulted. There must be . . . there must be . . . there must be another way.

Bessie F came down with flu or something else disabling. Her multiplication tables were badly singed by fever. She wept for the loss of one.

"Which one is gone?" asked Tessa.

The sufferer sobbed: "The sevenses."

"I think you've forgotten," said Mabel Chum. "You never had the sevenses. Not since you've been with us."

Then they brought her a cup of tea and assured her she'd never had them.

"Oh, pooh!" said Mabel Chum. "Nobody needs the sevenses. Besides, they have those things you hold that come with brains inside them. It's punchety punch and you have it." She couldn't recall the name.

But Bessie said they were dangerous. They gave off radiation. She relapsed into a series of coughs like a cat expelling a hair ball. Then she wept for her dentures. She couldn't recall where she kept them.

"We could look for them," said Mabel Chum, "but what are you planning to chew?"

Clearly, writing the checks was out, so Tessa was sent to Greeley. Each of the ladies concealed her age, but Tessa was deemed to be youngest. Anyway, she was given tasks, and she was careful to do them. Her spouse had ordered her about and she had learned compliance.

Greeley was mending a porch step when Tessa accosted him. "Mrs. Fortescue has come down with flu. Do you think you could pay a bill or two?" She was pleased to hear she was making a poem. "Or three or four or several more? There," she said. "I've never made a poem before."

He laughed aloud and drew out a pen clipped to his leather jacket. "Bring 'em on," he invited her. He made a boxing gesture as if he would knock them cold.

He sat on the steps and wrote them all with a flourish of his pen. "You're sure there is money to cover these?"

"Mrs. Fortescue says there is."

"And shall I write one for myself?"

"If you'll be good enough," she said.

She watched him as he wrote it out. "Don't you have another name?"

"Nope. It's Greeley, all it is."

"Well," she said, "you seem to be doing all right with it."

His eyes were the eyes of friendship. "What are you in for?" he asked her.

She looked confused.

"Well, this isn't a home for unwed mothers. So what is it a home for?"

"Oh," she said. ""Well, we all have leaky memories, and none of us can cope."

He laughed aloud. "Your memory has sprung a leak. Now, I find that appealing. I had a wife who could recall every damn thing I'd ever done."

"Do you miss her much?" she inquired.

"Not her memory I don't."

Tessa reflected, but not aloud, that most of her husband had leaked away.

"I like your hair," he ventured. "It bubbles like champagne."

"It's not supposed to bubble. It met with an accident."

He laughed again.

Just at that moment there came a terrible ruckus in back. Bessie Fortescue had come with a sleek black and white feline, one Muriel by name, even less amiable than Bessie herself and a thorn in the flesh to the Teasdale Persian named Honey Bun. Muriel devoured more food than her share. She snarled a lot. She was arrogant. Somewhere in the coils of her catty brain were doubtless encoded a few of the tables up through five and the capital cities worth a meow. But in Muriel's past Honey Bun sniffed an alley cat. Honey Bun knew that she owned the place, knew that she paid the bloody taxes. She was not about to take anything off an interloper, an alley cat. There was civil war.

"Oh, dear!" said Tessa. "That happens a lot."

"Do you want me to stop it?" Greeley asked.

"If you would be so good," she said.

So Greeley filled the bucket he kept beside the outside faucet. She watched him swing the bucket along as if it were filled with . . . nothing. In no time at all she heard the yowls. She felt herself in the car wash, again assaulted by water. She touched the bubbles of champagne hair.

There was silence.

When Greeley returned she smiled and sighed in a feminine way, "I wonder if you would accompany me."

"Where?" he asked.

"To the car wash."

He gave her the broadest smile. "Now, that's a proposal that's new to me."

"It's just that it makes me so afraid. There's so much water and so much soap. And I can't remember to get it right. They used to come out with brushes and pails."

"And now they leave it up to you."

"Yes," she said, "it's what they do."

"And they charge you more for it," he said. "I'm your man. Shall we go now?"

He put the checks into her hand. "Now, put these down in plain sight. We'll need your keys."

She let him drive and soon they were there. Even with Greeley beside her now, she found that she was a little afraid. When the water fell and the rivers of soap and the brushes that seemed to come down from God, she closed her eyes to let them pass. The car braced itself and shook. Suddenly her hand was held and squeezed in someone else's hand. She did not open her eyes to look. It must be Greeley's. It had to be. She thought she maybe should free her hand, and then she thought she wouldn't. In emergencies . . . in emergencies you hold a helping hand. And soon she was feeling young again and back in the swing on her front porch. She couldn't remember who else was there. She recalled the feeling but not the name. It seemed to be Greeley then and now.

That very night she dreamt about the granite moustache of Greeley. Once she touched it in her dream and found it softer than it looked. But still it looked like a tombstone. She strained her eyes to read the name.

THE CLEANLINESS of her Buick henceforth was much on Tessa's mind. And after another inspection, she inquired softly of Greeley if he could find the time. . . . "If I could watch you one more time, the way you punch those numbers."

"You bet," he said. "I'm all yours."

Without further ado they went. She studied his technique of punching. "I see," she said. "It's easy."

"Easy as pie," he told her. "But it takes a little practice before I want you on your own."

"It isn't just the numbers."

"I know," he said. "I'm with you."

"It always seems to me," she said, "I'm embarked upon a voyage. A storm comes up and I'm sinking fast. I have to pray an awful lot."

"Save your prayers. You're with me," he said.

When the storm came down in its fury, he circled her shoulders with an arm and very gently pressed them. The early days of her courtship came over her with a bang. And when the wash was over, they lingered a little longer, the way one does when the storm has passed but it's best to be sure of it. A storm has been known to turn around and lash you with its tail.

At last a car behind them honked. And Greeley said, "We need to find another place, one that is not so busy."

FOR THE BETTER PART of the following week Greeley was busy digging holes. It was a wonder to see him, how the hard earth would melt for him as if it were driven snow.

Then one night Tessa could not sleep. At last she rose and left her room and softly opened the door. Once outside in the cool night air, with only a streetlight to guide her, she drew herself a pail of water and tossed it onto the rump of her car, and then she filled the pail to the brim with Greeley's freshly driven dirt, and then she tossed it at her car, and then went back to bed.

She was a little ashamed, it's true, but it felt good to have done a thing for the first time in many a year that she deserved a spanking for.

The following day when Greeley came, he knocked and asked to speak to her. "Something has come up," he said. "It looks a little like trick or treat."

She thought his eye gave a little wink, as if he knew it wasn't so. He led her out to see her car.

"Oh, dear," she said in a voice of shock. "Whoever could have done this?"

"Boys," he said. "We should lock 'em up the minute they're born and this would never happen. But it can be fixed in no time. Of course I could save you some money and hose it down myself. What do you think?" he asked her.

She circled the car and pondered it. "I think it needs a scrub-bing," she said.

So off they went to the car wash. This time she leaned across him to punch the numbers herself. She brushed his Crusader scar hiding under his checkered shirt, and at once she was struck with a tender shock. Oh, dear, she thought. Oh, dear.

He clapped his hands to applaud her. "You're on your way," he told her. "Soon you won't be needing me." He gave her a definite winkety wink.

And when the rain came barreling down, this time Greeley kissed her. It seemed to her the finest kiss that she had ever experienced, though admittedly she could not recall the kisses of her past. The waters that fountained around them sprang from the fountain of youth. And his moustache was just as soft, as soft as she had dreamt it.

"I suppose you think me shameless," she said when they emerged. The drops that clung to her windshield were diamonds in the sun.

"Not a bit of it," he said. And then he said, "I'm thinking this didn't get it all. As long as we're here we should run her through another time, just to be safe about it."

THAT NIGHT she dreamed of his moustache. As ever, it looked like a tombstone, one for a lurking Turk. But when she strained to read the name, lo! it was her husband's name. Oh, dear, she thought, Oh, dear, oh, dear. Had she ever wished him dead?

THE CAR grew progressively dirtier, what with the drippings from the tree and the dust blown in from God knows where and the cat that lounged upon its hood and tracked it up with dirty paws, no doubt the Fortescue feline.

Mabel Chum grew suspicious. "What are you trying to prove?"

she asked. "It isn't good for a car, you know, to have a layer of skin washed off. The soap they use is very harsh. The brushes give it acne pits."

"Besides," said Bessie Fortescue, "we're all paying for Greeley's time. Why does he have to accompany you?"

"It's hard to explain," said Tessa.

AFTER A SEASON of washes, Tessa emerged in her Sunday best to announce that soon she was moving out. "Greeley and I are married."

They were struck to the bone with shock.

"I hope you'll be happy for me."

Mabel Chum began to chant: "I smelled it, I smelled it."

Ethel Malone began to weep. "My husband did everything for me. He lifted every burden."

"Dry up, Ethel!" said Bessie F. "He did every damn little damn little thing and how could we forget it?" She turned at once to Tessa. "This is exceedingly tacky of you. Now we must all pay higher rents."

"But you won't have me to feed, you know, and Greeley might take a little less."

"Less! Less!" cried Bessie F. "He's fired! Fired! Fired! My dear, he's after your money. It's as plain as the nose on your face."

"I don't have any money. It all goes out to you in rent."

"The fault is mine," said Mabel Chum. "You took her in on my say-so. But I think we need not go so far as to say we must lose our linchpin."

Ethel Malone was mopping her eyes. "Will someone please explain to me what a linchpin is?"

"Your husband, dear!" cried Bessie F. "When he fell out your wheel came off."

Baby Doll's eyes never left the bride. "Are you dressed for your honeymoon? Your navy is more becoming."

And Doll Baby followed it up: "Where will you go?" she wondered.

"Niagara Falls," said Tessa.

"Tacky! Tacky!" cried Bessie F. "Niagara has no class at all. Why would you want to go there? Is Greeley skulking out in the yard? Why doesn't he come and face us?"

But Tessa shook their dust from her feet and went to join her skulker.

Judgment Day

It might be out of the run of things to buy a house made out of a church, though nothing you'd call exceptional. It would have been smarter to rent perhaps, but Brian had had enough of apartments, and this was really the only house in the small New England town for sale. When he pondered his recent dry spell with the writing, he thought it was due, well, possibly due to the feeling of rank impermanence that pervaded his soul — his spirit, whatever. He did not much believe in his soul. He'd begun to feel he was passing through. . . . Passing through what? And that, of course, he was leaving unanswered.

So he summoned his wife of eleven years, who was thoroughly sick of apartment living and had gone for a long sojourn with her mother. They had seemed of late somewhat less than married, and this perhaps was her reason for leaving. Now catching the lively note in his voice, she decided he might be fun to live with. She hadn't minded his hours of writing. When he was at it, wherever his thought, she felt included, felt vaguely needed. It was the hours he gazed into space — and these were becoming a generous portion of every day — that locked her out. Wiped her out, she wanted to say. As if he were back in those distant parts he'd traveled in before they met.

They converged on the house from different directions, she from Connecticut, he from New York. They arrived at almost the very same time on a fairish day the end of June.

"Have you already bought it?" Her name was Alice.

"Of course not," he said. "I wouldn't do that before you'd seen it."

"That's nice," she said. She was small and blonde and softly featured, with the sort of face a man could summon and come to wonder why he had. Her eyes were blue and obedient. Before she had put her contacts in, she couldn't see a blessed thing. And when they were in, she saw no more than she wanted to see, unless requested to see some more.

"You said on the phone it's Anglican. My mother was one before she married, but Daddy didn't believe in it." She was a sweetly diligent woman on the brink of forty — Brian was older, forty-eight — but she gave the impression of indolence, for she had the knack of appearing freshly bathed and anointed, however vigorous her day.

It still looked very much like a church, the cruciform shape of it intact. The modest belfry was bereft of its bell, but they couldn't see that from where they stood. The painters had done it all in green — a secular green, which they labeled "fern" and which blended nicely with all the spruce — and added shutters and painted them brick.

"I'd like the shutters better white. Why would they sell a church?" she asked.

He was backing away to get perspective. "The realtor, a Mr. Turnbull, says that over the years the congregation moved away and those who were left couldn't keep it up. They drive to a bigger church somewhere. They like to get in their cars and go.

Have Sunday dinner out of town. The village is really pretty small."

"How small?" said Alice.

"I didn't ask. Because I'm not opening a grocery store. But look around." Alice would always go into statistics. "Turnbull says the residents are very keen on keeping it small. I thought that was what we wanted," he said.

And the church was small, as churches go. The tiny narthex was now a foyer. The nave of course was the living room, soaring thirty-five feet or so, with dark crossbeams in the vaulted roof and hanging lights and pointed windows. The old stained glass had been removed. A strip of carpet, crimson as some exotic bird, stretched the entire length of the room. The floors gleamed dark on either side. "The original flooring, according to Turnbull. All heartwood, according to him. Dry rot or something claimed the rest, so they tore it down and built it back, oh, sixty years or so ago. Before the Depression hit, he said. So everything is up to snuff. The carpet will have to go, of course."

"It's a little red but not too bad. What have they done with the pews?" she asked.

"Well, one of them is in the foyer. I expect they sold the rest for cash. Aren't they always looking for cash?"

"Is there such a thing as a churchyard sale?" She was feeling glad. She squinted up at the vaulted top. "How do we get the cobwebs down?"

He was feeling rather good himself. There was nothing said, but they separately knew, and together knew, that this was another chance for them. Before they met he had traveled to various parts of the world, in the main remote, looking for things to seed his mind and harvest if they took root and grew. He had strained so long to catch so much that his eyes were losing their power to see what was useful to him and what was not. He felt like a child in blindman's bluff who is scarfed and twirled till he's lost his way.

He had married her roots and her way of seeing just so much. Marriage had turned the trick for him. For a while . . . till he found he wanted more. Till he longed to try his eyes again. He had failed to keep her from finding out. Though he never saw them, he felt her tears.

"Cobwebs?" he said. "Who'd ever see 'em? If it's guests you mean, the carpet will strike them blind and deaf."

The transepts had both been turned into bedrooms with doors to cut them off from the nave. She could not get over how clever it was. At the rear on the left a door led into the breakfast room-kitchen and one on the right to a bedroom, a nursery, a storage room, whatever you wanted, the realtor had said. Both were narrow and looked out over the garden plot.

Nestled between these rooms was his study, a tiny room but with space enough for his desk, he saw. A generous window, newly cut, looked over the little garden. The same red carpet covered the floor. High on the wall a square-cut pane of colored glass let in a vivid reddish light.

"I'm not sure about that light," he said.

"Nonsense," she said, her voice with a lilt. "Your books are inclined to be gloomy, you know. This will probably lighten them up."

"It's news to me you think they're gloomy."

She waved her hand. "Gloomy in spots was all I meant."

"Life is gloomy in spots," he said.

She did not want to go into that. "Let's take it," she said. "I like it a lot. And it's such a bargain." She looked around with a little smile. "It will be a challenge, don't you think? Living in a church. We shall have to turn from our wicked ways."

He laughed at that. "Let's not," he said. He slanted his eyes at the carpet below. "This rug will have to go," he said. "Here and in there."

"You mean the color. I guess you're right."

But when they were all moved in that August and he brought the carpet up again, she flatly stated she wanted to wait. "Till we can afford what we really want. When you finish the book and get your advance. . . . Let's not rush in where angels wouldn't fear to tread."

"It's not a church," he reminded her. Her pointless humor left him cold. "It's a house . . . a house. A house is a house is a house."

"Still . . . ," she said but didn't finish.

He had been surprised that she seemed to like the house a lot. He had thought he would have to push it a bit. He was happy at first, with a kind of boyish anticipation. He was glad to be away from the city. He had put off writing until he was settled. They took long walks in the afternoons through woods and fields. She bought a book at the local store that helped her to name the flowers they found. She filled the house with bunches of them. "They keep the eye from the rafters," she said.

He used to be good with a hammer and saw and found he had not forgotten his skill. He built her boxes for white petunias and pink begonias and shelves to hold them to the rear of the house. And of course there were shelves for the kitchen walls. They were both surprised to find her domestic. She purchased berries from roadside trucks and put them up into jars she bought. And while she worked she hummed a tune he couldn't recall having heard before. It was always the same, a stately measure. She hummed it as if she were thinking the words. Sometimes he could see them in her eyes as she raised a glass of preserves to the light. But he did not know or ask the words.

The garden in back had gone to ruin. He spent long hours in setting it straight, hacking away at the honeysuckle that choked the herbs and the morning glories that stitched together the hollyhocks, which must, he supposed, have reseeded themselves. There were some splendid laurel shrubs that he spent a week in shaping

well. And rangy lilacs past their prime that he pruned and nour-
ished for next year's bloom. He found an unexpected treasure, a
well-established asparagus bed. He assumed it had been there for
many years. Periwinkle had covered the roots and had to be carefully plucked away. Honeysuckle had claimed the stalks and had
to be scrupulously unwound. The apple trees looked promising
but needed the proper spray, he guessed, whenever he got around
to them.

It was in so hacking, unwinding, and pruning, with a kind of
nervous, tight-lipped vigor, that he came upon the open graves not
fifty feet beyond the house. There were holes, a dozen of them,
which a careless hand had filled with soil. But the soil had settled,
and now they were basins to hold the rain and mirror the sky and
mirror his face as he leaned above them to tear the cover of vines
away. He would hardly have known what he'd come across if it had
not been for the bits of granite, shards of headstones with rem-
nants of chiseled dates and names.

He could not really account for his shock. He turned away and
called to his wife, who was potting begonias. She came with her
hands in garden gloves and a smudge of wet loam across her cheek.
"We've bought an abandoned graveyard," he said. "I could throw
the damn thing in Turnbull's face!"

She peered into one of the cavities. "Why?" she said. "What did
you expect? People get buried around a church."

"It doesn't bother you in the least?"

"Why should it?" she asked. She would often parry his question
with hers, a habit he had never liked. "I suppose they're moved to
another church." She looked at him with serene and faintly humor-
ous eyes. "Well, they couldn't sell us the people, could they? Isn't
it better to move them away?"

"I didn't bargain for any of this."

She was following the line of low granite stones that formed the enclosure. And then she stopped. "Look," she said, "here's one that's left." She dropped to her knees, brushing away the dirt and vines. "It's a man named Joseph Jones. 1868 to 1916." She read aloud, "'Here lies the body of Joseph Jones. May he be cursed who moves my bones.'" She looked up, wondering. "Well, that explains it . . . why he wasn't moved."

"God!" he said.

He drove straight in and accosted Turnbull.

"You have me confused. What is your complaint?" The matey, helpful manner was gone. "You can't have wanted the people left. There's a law against it, anyway. If the boys were careless about filling the holes — I expect it rained and settled the dirt — I'll send them out tomorrow some time and have the spot filled in and smoothed."

"Are you aware that one is left?"

"Well, yes, there's one that couldn't be moved. At least nobody wanted to do it. People are skittish about these things. Moving somebody don't want to be moved. If it's in a will they couldn't care less, but carved on a stone is something else."

"So you're just going to leave him buried there."

"I'm afraid that's so. If you want to go into it legally . . . get the court's permission to dig him up. But then you'll have to put him somewhere, and get permission for where you put him, and that's the law. But the Church will probably have lots to say."

Brian turned on his heel and left.

He left the cavities just as they were. Nobody arrived to fill them in. He had lost his taste for the garden, he found. The thought occurred that he worked in the garden, made boxes for plants, or went for walks because it kept him away from his study. When he understood this to be the case, he took himself quite firmly in hand and walked the length of the living room — he always fell into a measured tread down the crimson way, as if caught

up in some kind of procession — and entered his study and sat at
his desk, his back to the window as well as the garden, and quite
deliberately took up his pen.

He became aware of a certain oppression. Something a little
like childish dread. The feeling of being awash in sorrow and thinking it would have no end. It was very faint, like a distant echo. The
room itself, though miniature, seemed unaccountably full of
space. He forced himself to scan the wall to assure himself that the
room was small. An interesting trick of the mind, he thought.

Once when he traveled in India he had entered a tiny temple
at dusk. The walls, he could tell, were painted with figures, but the
light was too dim to tell what they were. He made his way to the
center of the room and turned and turned as he strained to see,
and suddenly the walls receded. The figures seemed to shrink with
distance. The room itself was full of sky. He had stumbled out and
gone his way.

But that was India, a different land. Whatever it was, you didn't
take it back with you. You didn't let it into your house.

He forced his eyes to the paper now. The contact served to
reassure him. But the crimson carpet was in his eyes, and just
beyond lay a square of light like a splash of wine where the reddish glow from the pane in the wall was lying upon the carpet red.

He told his wife he was ripping the carpet up in his study. And
he went about it with resolution, tossing the whole of it into the
trash. There was mold on the underlying boards, so down on his
hands and knees he scrubbed. He scrubbed the boards into a bur-
nished gray and then surveyed them with satisfaction. Again he
seated himself at his desk. The light from the pane on his bare
wood floor was the splash of a different sort of wine. Port, he
decided. A ruby port. Through his study wall he could hear his wife
humming away at her usual song above the shrill of running water.

He got up and went to the kitchen door. She saw him and

smiled and went on with her work. She was washing lettuce.
"Alice," he said, "what *is* that song . . . the one you hum?"

She looked surprised and thought for a moment. "Just now?"
she said. The afternoon sun was in her hair.

"Just now and always."

She laughed a bit. "I guess it's 'The Church's One Foundation.'
I don't always hum it."

He heard her words with sharp distaste. "Yes, you do. Why do
you hum it?"

"I'm sure I hum some other hymns."

"Why must you always hum a hymn? You never did before we
came."

She looked perplexed. "Well, I really don't know. Why does it
matter?"

"It drives me nuts."

"Good Lord," she said. "Imagine that. . . . I must have gotten it
from my mother. I suppose it just comes naturally. Living in a
church, all of that."

"This isn't a church. It's a house," he said. He couldn't stand the
way she was giving in to the place.

He returned to his desk. But the sound of her hymn would not
release him. Behind him a dozen open graves proclaimed his own
mortality.

He went for a walk alone in the woods. The trail was a carpet
of princess pine. It muffled his step and left him insubstantial as
rain, as the resinous scent his foot released. Turning back, he
sought his study, and grimly he began to write: Chapter Five of the
book in progress months ago. It had to do with an expedition lost
in the Alps. Once in Zermatt he had heard the story, and now he
was making a fiction of it. All the details he had finely imagined.
It was the sort of thing he could do. The feel of the snow, the light
on the peaks, the haunted nights, the savor of hope, the worm of

despair. He forced himself to recapture the scene, recalling the winter month in Zermatt, the looming presence of the Matterhorn.

But his mind unaccountably drifted from it into a scene half a world away, one he had not thought of for years and even at the time had thought little about. He had been traveling for days in Burma and had heard of a festival on his route. In the midst of a famine they could celebrate! Or perhaps because of the famine they could, treading their hunger into the ground. He had stationed himself by the main thoroughfare to watch the procession, when abruptly a small woman dashed from the crowd and lifted to him a small brown baby. He was used to giving alms when accosted. Mechanically he had reached for a coin. She signed to him to hold the child while she put the fifty-cent piece away. Trying to conceal his awkwardness, he took the baby into his arms, and at once she turned and dashed away. For an instant he was too stunned to move, but then he endeavored to follow her. She had lost herself in the milling crowd. His search was useless, he presently saw, and at last he looked at the child in his arms, a little boy — a few months old, it was hard to tell. The great brown eyes were old and trusting. He had never seen such trusting eyes. The lips were the shape of a tiny plum. But the arms that grasped his neck were frail and the folded legs were a tangle of bones. He was swept along by the surging crowd till he saw an old and wizened man, a loincloth about his hips, who sat cross-legged with a heap of sticks. With corded hands extended as if to a feeble blaze, he was shielding the sticks from the tramping feet. Brian had shifted the boy in his arms and drawn two dollar bills from his pocket. He handed the bills and the child to the man and, like the woman, passed into the crowd.

Now sitting at his familiar desk with the splash of red on the floor before him, it seemed to him that he would weep. It seemed to him that his life had crested and fallen then, and why this was so he could not say. When, years before, he had lost himself in that alien throng, he had lost himself. . . . He was filled with grief that he and Alice had no child. He had never grieved for the lack before. In fact he had counted it fortunate. It was clear to him now he deserved no child.

My God, he thought, it's this damnable place. He got up and found his wife in the yard. She was saying goodbye to a Mrs. Hiller, who lived down the road. A wind had risen and was stirring the grass. The middle-aged woman, her head in a scarf, waved to him and walked away. The wind was whipping the ends of her scarf. Her short, spare figure, her rapid walk, for a moment put him in mind of someone . . . the woman who had lost herself in the crowd. Or was it himself . . . who like the woman had walked away?

Alice turned with a welcoming smile. "Mrs. Hiller used to go to this church. . . ." She pursed her lips. "This house when it used to be a church. She says your study is right where the sanctuary used to be . . . where the altar was. The red pane of glass was above the altar. She says Father Damon, who was priest here for years, she says he was fond of telling them that every altar is the center of the earth. Isn't that nice? I like it, don't you?"

He stared at her with incredulous eyes. How could she possibly think he would like it? Was she wholly lacking in empathy? Sometimes it appeared that her mind was scrubbed as totally clean as the rest of her always appeared to be. Was her innocent-seeming persistence a cloak for some resentment that festered within? He began to fear that from the start he and his wife had been mismatched and that each could only wound the other.

That night she slept at peace beside him, stirring a little, smiling a little, while he lay awake and thought of the graves. He went to sleep as dawn was breaking.

At breakfast she said, "You know what I dreamt? I dreamt that man, that Joseph Jones, who is still out there, came into our room and looked at us. And you know what he said? He said, 'There is no giving in marriage in heaven.' I think that's in the Bible, isn't it?"

"I wouldn't know. I'm an unbeliever."

"There's really no such thing," she said.

"A ghost or an unbeliever?" he asked.

"Both, I guess."

"You guess?"

"I guess. Brian," she said, "you mix me up. Does it give you pleasure?"

"I assure you I'm not having fun."

"Well, I'm not having any fun either."

They left it at that.

And yet she did seem to be having fun. She took up the garden where he'd left it off and gossiped down the road with the neighbors and drank their cups and cups of tea. He went for walks in the woods without her.

But on these solitary walks a troubling thing began to occur. He would often hear the sound of a bell, very distant, very faint, a measured, mournful, tolling knell. He found himself walking in time to it. Whenever he paused in the bird-filled shade he noted the tolling would pause as well. One day when Alice was down the road he got the ladder and mounted the rear of the house outside and climbed through the opening into the attic. From there he could see the door to the belfry. The hempen rope was hanging through. He pulled and it fell with a thud at his feet. A ladder was fastened against the wall. He tugged until he got it loose. Then he climbed and opened the small trapdoor. The bell was gone, as he knew it would be. Turnbull had said the bell was gone.

He did not mention the thing to Alice, but he broached the subject of taking up the living room carpet.

"You think so?" she said, a little line between her eyes. "I thought we were going to wait for your money."

"Look," he said, "I'll do all the work. I'll scrub the boards and stain them to match the ones at the side, and then we can throw some cheap little rugs, two or three of them, around. It won't look bare, I promise you. And when the money comes rolling in, we'll get the whole thing carpeted."

"Men are supposed to like red," she said. "All the men I know like red."

"Well, this particular shade of red seems to require a whacking chorus."

"A hymn," she said.

He did not reply.

He went to work with the stripping and scrubbing. It was strenuous work. He was on the attack. After two weeks he returned to his study and grimly settled down to write. Each word for him was an act of defiance. And after several hours of this, exhausted, he went for a walk through the town — he had given up the walks in the woods — then returned and read over what he had written. He was stunned. The delicacy of his touch was gone. He had written the stormy night at the inn. A coarseness pervaded the scene of love. Vulgarity was a better term.

I'm fighting this room, he grew aware. I'm pushing too hard. It will ruin me. He stared at the square of light on the floor, which the afternoon sun gave the color of blood. He thought of the child with the trusting eyes he had bought in Burma for fifty cents and reckoned how old he would be today. Fifteen years and seven months . . . and fourteen days . . . and added to that his age at the time. If he's still alive, which he doubtless isn't. The child I bought for fifty cents and turned and dumped for a couple of bucks. And here I sit in the center of the earth . . . with a corpse in my garden and a child who is dead because of me. And in a few years I too shall be dead, and what will have been the point of my life?

He stood up and paced the tiny room, stepping over the square of light, which seemed to shift and faintly to quiver. He felt aloof from the house and his wife. He could hear her through the wall between, running water, preparing supper. But it was as if she were quite remote. He could not quite remember her face.

He recalled instead his brother's face. A time he had taken his brother fishing because his mother had said he must and how he had locked him up in a shed just before they reached the lake and how his brother had cried with fear. Each step of the way to the shore of the lake he had heard the sobs. He remembered the suck of the marshy earth and the faint whistle of water reeds and the cry of gulls between the sobs. He had caught a fish and then returned to let him out. The face was grimed with dirt and tears. "You can have my fish if you won't tell." His brother had taken his fish in silence and then had thrown it into the lake. And now the small face disappeared with a tiny click inside his mind. He was left with a vague, insufferable pain.

He emerged to announce they would sell the house. "I simply cannot handle it here. I'm falling apart." He sat and put his face in his hands.

For the first time she really seemed to hear him. She paused with a boning knife in her hand. "Oh, dear," she said, her blue eyes budding with her dismay. Her hands were red from peeling beets. "Whatever you say, but I liked it here." Already she placed it in the past.

He noted it and was grateful to her. "You're different," he said. "You don't fight the place."

She considered this. "You're a writer," she said. "You imagine things more."

"I've been a writer since I was ten and I never came up with stuff like this." He was grateful she did not ask him what. "You believe in God. You believe in a church."

She brushed the hair from her troubled eyes with the hand that held the boning knife. "I don't think I do."

"Well, you must believe without knowing it."

Distressed, she seemed to probe herself.

"Do put down that knife," he said.

"Listen," she said, "Mrs. Hiller said something. She said the church was never deconsecrated before it was sold." She watched him hopefully. "I'm not making this up. She said when a church stops being a church they have a ceremony of deconsecration. The bishop told Father Damon to do it, and he said he would but he didn't, she said."

He stared at her. "Why didn't he?"

"She doesn't know. She thought it was maybe an oversight. . . . Brian," she said, "let's get it done."

"I'd feel like a goddamn fool," he said.

She nodded her head. "Let's do it anyway."

"Why should it make any difference," he said, "if he comes and says some mumbo-jumbo? I don't believe in any of it."

"Look," she said, blue eyes aroused, "it might be something like Halloween. I mean it," she said. "You all take off to the haunted house. There's nothing there but everybody says there is. For maybe years and years they do, and so you do and you really feel. . . ."

"Alice," he said, "I'm not a child, and I don't believe in any of this."

"But all those people who came here did."

"But they're not here now. We're here now and we don't believe. So please put down that bloody knife." He hated the tone he took with her. He wished she wouldn't stand for it. She always turned the other cheek.

Before they went to bed she said, "I'll ask Mrs. Hiller where he went."

The following day at lunch she reported: "Mrs. Hiller says he has a church at Corinth. He's written to her and she has his address."

"That's a good fifty miles away."

"We'll go," she said. "We'll go tomorrow." When she rose to take his plate away, she leaned and kissed the top of his head. He was the child she reassured.

Over her coffee and cake she yawned. "I dreamt about that man again. He's rather nice but lots of beard. He just came in and looked at us and said, 'My stone is getting warm.' I suppose he meant his tombstone."

"Alice," he said, "if you have a rendezvous with Jones, I really don't care to hear of it."

"You're jealous," she said. "That's very nice."

THEY ATE THEIR BREAKFAST and left at nine. The day was fine, with sun enough to lighten the heart and a sheen of dew on the meadows they passed. She was wearing her Sunday best, he noted; his dress was intentionally casual. He supposed that much could be made of this, but he didn't care to go into it. As they drove he said, "I think I've marshaled my thoughts a bit, so before we get there I want you to know where I've come with it."

She drew her eyes from the road to him.

"Inside, we're most of us a mess."

She pondered it. "I never thought of myself that way."

"That's because you're less of a mess."

"Thank you, Brian."

He quietly groaned. "When I pay you a compliment I'll let you know."

Her eyes upon him filled with tears. "I take whatever I can get."

He took her hand, his eyes on the road. "I promise you this. If we can get over this thing at the house, I'll be a helluva lot more fun."

She drew a breath.

He tried to go on. "We all have a past. We have things in our minds we refuse to recall . . . ways and times and people we failed.

I think I may have been working up to where I am at the present time. This place where we live is remarkably also a place in my mind . . . that is, my life. And something about the past of the house. . . ."

"You're sure it's not the present of the house?" He released her hand. "Because if it isn't, what are we going to Corinth for?"

He drove for a while. "I guess I'm not sure of a bloody thing. But I'm not giving this fellow an inch. What do we call him?" he wanted to know.

"Mrs. Hiller calls him Father Damon."

"I don't think I can manage the Father. Is Damon his first or his last name?"

"Brian, I haven't the foggiest notion. We'll call him Sir. You can't really ever go wrong with Sir."

They found him at the rear of his church in a clerical collar and rolled-up sleeves. He was picking golf balls out of the grass. When they appeared he straightened up. He proved to be short and slight of frame with a florid, somewhat freckled face and reddish hair in disarray. His eyes were small and made of steel. They seemed to dismiss whatever you thought and yet they seemed to want to know. Alice decided she'd never discuss her life with him, but he might be fun to picnic with.

"I've warned them," he said. "I've returned the last they'll ever get. Anything over the hedge is mine. . . . Do you play?" he asked. "If you do, I make you a present of these. They buy the best." And he held them out, five balls in his hand like a setting of eggs.

They shook their heads.

"A pity," he said. "Well, I'll pop them into the mission box." He turned and led them toward a rear church door. "You're the happy couple with the baby needs 'doing.' In England they 'have the baby done.' Perhaps you knew. Three weeks from Sunday I'm down for christenings. An exceptionally fertile parish, you know. Your only child?" He turned to them.

"Quite another matter," said Brian and introduced himself and Alice. "If we could trouble you for a moment."

"Of course, of course. Come in, come in. I was expecting a brace of parents." He led them into a small bright office with bamboo blinds that sliced the sunlight into shreds. On a stand beside his desk was a large stuffed mallard with wings outspread. "A gift," he said and patted its head. "Some of the faithful are lovers of birds and shoot them down whenever they can." Next door someone was typing away at a reckless clip. He waved them into white cane chairs with flowered pads and sat himself behind the desk. He unrolled his sleeves and fastened the cuffs and looked at Brian with curious eyes. "Are you perhaps a member here? I'm a recent thing, and parts of the flock keep strolling in just when I think I've counted them all."

Brian waited. "I'm not a member of any church. Nor do I believe in God," he said.

Alice wished he wouldn't be so up front.

"I see," said Damon. "A full-time thing? Sundays and holidays off perhaps? Most of my flock take Sundays off. And are you employed with anything else?"

"I'm a fiction writer."

"A fiction writer! Yes, indeed," His bright eyes snapped. "Are you pretty good?"

"I used to be, but not any more."

"And that, I suppose, is why you're here. Perhaps you need a psychiatrist. A mental therapist, we call it now. I have a splendid agnostic friend, gets himself hypnotized once a month and then he produces all manner of art. He's filled the courthouse walls with murals."

Brian eyed him coldly. The typist was rollicking across the page.

Thoughtfully Damon stroked the mallard. "Well, I see you don't fancy a mental therapist. So how can I be of service to you?"

"We have bought a house that was once your church."

"Ah . . . h!" said the priest, leaning back in his chair with a shrieking of springs. "I knew it would sell. A lovely location. Southern exposure. One of the transept windows is loose. It rattles a bit when the wind is high. The garden of course needs tidying up."

"The garden contains some open graves. And one that is still inhabited."

"Pardon me, when you say open graves, it does suggest grave robbers at work — the bodies inside and sadly exposed. These bodies have been removed, of course, removed to consecrated ground."

"This brings me," said Brian, "to why I am here. I understand that you failed to deconsecrate the church before it became this home of mine. I ask you to correct the oversight."

Damon got up and took a turn behind his desk and adjusted a blind. "Well, well, well." The typist was rattling like one possessed. He walked to her door. "Cordelia, my dear, why don't we give the machine a rest? Find something that's dry and water it. Or something that squeaks and give it some oil." The typing ceased. He returned to his desk and sat down again. "So that's how it is. Someone has let the cat out of the bag. It was not, I may say, an oversight."

"An act of disobedience, perhaps?"

"Precisely that. Precisely that." He smoothed his ruffled hair a bit and then he raked it the other way. "And if I don't come and put it to rights, you'll tell the bishop on me, eh? Just let me jot down his name and address. His telephone number may be of use. He's in his office after ten but takes a nap from one to three. A touch of asthma. Advised to rest."

"Oh, no," said Alice, becoming alarmed. "We wouldn't do that. We truly wouldn't."

"I like to arouse the bishop," said Damon. "It gives him pleasure to be aroused. And then he forgives me ten times over. It makes us both feel closer to God. It helps his asthma a bit, I think. Just what is the problem you have?" he said. "It can't be a theological one."

Brian was ready. "It resonates."

The steel-gray eyes grew wide at that. "A wonderful word . . . it 'resonates.' A fiction writer's word, I'm sure. I confess I don't know what it means."

Brian did not flinch. "It's haunted," he said.

"You mean that Joseph Jones out back?"

"No, I don't mean that." And he looked at the wall. "It's not a haunting. It's more a judgment. And I don't want to be judged. Not yet. I want to get on with what I do, be crabby about it, whatever it takes, snap at my good wife now and then, forget the things I need to forget, forget about having to measure up, forget the edge of the cliff is there. When I finish up, then I can be judged."

"I see," said Damon after a pause. "You don't fancy being judged in the middle. Once a week perhaps on a Sunday, if you went to church, which of course you don't, but if you did you could stomach that. But every day, all day, all night, you just would like to be left alone."

"You seem to understand me," said Brian.

"I do," said Damon, "quite thoroughly. And yet I confess a small confusion. Who is it you think is judging you . . . since of course you don't believe in God?"

"I cannot answer that," said Brian.

"It could hardly be better put," said Damon. He turned to Alice. "And what about you, my dear?" he asked.

She looked abashed.

"Speak up," he said. "I must have your view."

"Well . . . ," she said, "I don't mind it there."

"It? You mean the holiness?"

She nodded faintly. "But I want to keep my marriage safe. More than anything else I know."

"And you think the holy endangers it?"

She nodded again. "I guess that's it. It's the way he feels. I guess that's it." She looked at Brian with tears in her eyes.

He took her hand.

"Let me ask you this: do you plan to live there the rest of your lives?"

"Who knows?" said Brian.

"We hope to," said Alice.

Damon swiveled a bit, drumming the tips of his fingers together. "You're making a big mistake," he said. "You've got a property that's fully protected. As much as any place can be. Better than any insurance you buy. No yearly payments. No thirty days' grace. You've got the grace as long as you live there. And you want to give that protection up?"

"I do," said Brian, "with all my heart."

Damon flipped a paper clip and caught it. "Well, then, you've got it. Or, I should say, you haven't got it. Shall we leave right now? Just give me a moment to find my book. Why don't you wait in your car?" he said. "I'll be along in just a minute."

They went outside and sat in their car. "I think he's kind of cute," said Alice.

"Cute?" he said. "I'd call him about as slick as they come."

She looked concerned. "If that's what he is . . . if that's all he is, do you think he can do it?"

"We'll see," he said.

"I think it just may rain," said Alice.

After some ten minutes or so they saw him sail from the side of the church. He was wearing a black cassock down to his heels and over his arm a snow white garment edged with lace and over the bush of his reddish locks a strange black hat like a sort of tam.

"Here comes our exorcist," said Brian.

"My goodness," said Alice, "he's going to do it right."

He waved to them, jumped into a battered green Toyota, and sped away from them down the street. "Of course he knows the way," said Alice.

He was already there when they arrived, paying his last respects to the graves. "Well, well," he said, when he saw them approach, "I see what you mean. It does look a bit like Judgment Day. The final trumpet and all of that. But a little unconsecrated dirt will put the place to rights again. The bishop might even bear the expense. I can't commit him. He's rather close. But in fact he has a discretionary fund, which is fatter, I think, than he cares to tell. I'll approach him when his asthma is right."

He teetered on the clods of earth, and once he tripped on the honeysuckle and knocked his hat a little askew. But he righted himself and made his way to Joseph Jones. He stood for a time in silence before him. His head was bowed.

"Poor old bastard," he said at last. He turned to Brian. "That's a term of affection. He *was* a bastard. I looked him up. He'd probably been shunted from pillar to post. He was captured by pirates and taken to sea, and now at the end he craves to remain in one peaceful spot till Judgment Day. One peaceful consecrated spot. You've read his inscription. I honor his wish. Even the gravediggers honored his wish." He sighed a little and crossed himself. "I grew to be very fond of Joseph. Because of him I didn't go through with deconsecration. I couldn't leave him high and dry. Surrounded by possible godlessness." He glanced at Brian from under his hat.

He cleared his throat. "Did you have a use for this spot of earth? The site of a bramble bush perhaps? Or one of those blooming althea things that never know when it's time to quit?"

Alice spoke up. "Oh, no, I think he should stay where he is. He gets in my dreams but I don't mind." She hesitated. "Do you think you could deconsecrate, well, everything else but leave his grave the way it is?"

Damon nodded. "A brilliant solution, one I was going to suggest myself. But only, of course, if your husband approves. For it seems he has purchased the bones of Jones and what little ground they occupy. If he feels his fiction career will suffer. . . . I mean to say he may want the whole thing totally sterile. He may be concerned that a few feet of holiness could spread. A heavy rain could redistribute the soil a bit. When he walks in the garden after that, in spots he might feel a twinge of judgment. However," he said, setting his hat to rights, "I could indeed petition containment." He sighed and looked again at the grave. "But He doesn't, you know, always answer my prayers."

"That will be satisfactory," said Brian. "I'm willing to compromise on that."

"Splendid!" said Damon. "And I in turn will commit you to nothing. No compact with the Divine of course. I shall leave you totally outside the fold."

"Thank you," said Brian.

"And you, my dear." He turned to Alice. "Do you wish to remain outside the fold?"

"I wish to remain with my husband," she said.

"A most courageous stand," said Damon. "A course not every wife could choose."

After that he turned and went round to the front. They followed him at a little distance. Clouds were massing overhead. At the door he shrugged into his garment with lace. He drew from the generous folds of his cassock a strip of black cloth that looked like a ribbon with which he proceeded to yoke himself. He drew out a book whose covers were red. Then he removed his hat and turned. "You may join me of course. I'm just presuming you pre-fer to wait."

"We do," said Brian. He took Alice's hand.

Damon opened the door and went inside.

"Do you think it's going to work?" said Alice. He didn't reply. "Well, if we think it will, it will."

"That may be what it comes to," he said.

A little wind blew up in the pines. A little thunder roared in the east. "I hope he gets through before it rains. . . . I feel so sorry for Joseph," she said. "I just may cry. It's all so sad." In a moment she asked, "Do we tip him, Brian?"

"Of course not," he said. "It's part of his job. And he should have done it before he left."

"Still, he's come such a lot of miles." The drops at once began to fall. She cut and ran round to the back of the house. She re-turned with a bulging paper sack and stood with it while it spot-ted with rain. He did not want to know what it was.

"You think we might stand in the foyer?" she asked. Her hair was beginning to hang in strings. "This is the very best suit I own."

"No!" he said. "It might put a crimp in his operation. I want him to do the whole damn place. Go sit in the car."

But she wouldn't desert. She stood her ground. "I guess the graves are filling up."

"Alice, you say the damnedest things."

When Damon emerged at last, she pressed upon him the sod-den bag. "This is a jar of my quince preserve. It was made while the house was . . . the way you left it."

Brian groaned within.

"Thank you, my dear. I shall eat it without the slightest qualm." He took it and restored the hat to his head.

Brian gestured toward the house. "Is it clean?" he asked.

"Clean?" said Damon, enduring the rain. "Well, it's open, I'd say.

Open to the devil and all his minions. You're going to have to keep careful watch."

Brian smiled. "You bet," he said. "And thank you, sir."

"I mean it," said Damon. "Be on your guard." And he tipped his hat, got into the car, waved to them once, and drove away.

"I wish he hadn't said that," said Alice.

"Nonsense," said Brian. "He's ribbing us. Come out of the rain."

"I don't think he was."

He put his arm around her then. "Don't tell me you believe in the devil."

"Of course I don't. But I think he does."

They walked inside. The rain was clattering overhead as if the typist was on the roof.

"It doesn't look any different," she said. "But it feels so . . . empty." Her voice was grave. "Do you think it's safe?"

The Great and Small

THERE WAS ONCE a little girl called Mara, who was born, they said, with the gift of prayer. She had other gifts: fine brown eyes that could toast your heart, like stretching your feet before the hearth, and a wonderful fall of midnight hair, which had a mind of its wonderful own. Her mother kept it pulled from her face and braided tightly down her back. But when she played it came gently loose and soon was like a glistening chain, and then the chain became unlinked, and then the links became a cloud, and then your heart grew warm again. But eyes and hair would pale beside her gift for prayer.

She lived in a village beside the sea. Every morning the fishing vessels went out for the day and then returned when the light would fade. The village women were much alone. Left to their children and to themselves, they pondered at leisure this gift of Mara's. The children first had put it to use. If a pet kitten or dog would sicken, Mara would put it to rights again. She stroked its head and closed her eyes and whispered a prayer no one could hear. Sometimes when a tiny baby grew sick, Mara would be called to help. And once when a baby came into the world and failed to breathe in spite of all, Mara was swept away from her game and hustled into the darkened room and given its tiny limp fingers to hold. She closed her eyes and moved her lips, and soon his fingers curled and tightened about her own. "He's breathing," they said in wondering tones, and then they told her she could leave. But Mara stayed because his hand wouldn't let her go. Now that he was beginning to walk, whenever Mara came in sight he seemed to remember how it had been and held her dress when she tried to leave.

No one had taught Mara how to pray, and she never told any-one how she did.

The winter had been hard that year. The wind had whipped the vessels about. The ice in the mornings coated their masts. For days they never went out at all. Their masts were a huddle of leafless trees. They were birds that had never made it south. The spring, when it came, was all the better for being the object of winter dreams. Who is to say that seasons are never subtly moved by the selfsame longing in every breast and a restlessness for the sea in boats and a sigh of memory that haunts the shore?

But spring brought with it more than joy. The houses were rocked with a rumor as cold as the winter wind. And then the rumor became a fact. At the foot of a bluff the fishermen dwelt and their boats rocked. Except that the boats were not theirs at all. They belonged to the man who bought their fish and sold it to inland cities and towns. The fish, of course, belonged to the sea. He lived at the very top of the bluff in a lordly house that none but the priest had been inside. Even the priest had not been asked but had traveled there in the way of duty and been admitted for courtesy's sake. The man of the house had sold the boats for a splendid price to someone who wanted them far from there. The entire fleet would be sailed away, and then how would the villagers live?

The little church was filled with prayers, but the word held: he would sell the fleet. The villagers were nothing to him. It was pleasant to see from his fine house his fishing vessels far out to sea, the sunlight glinting from stern and bow and making the mastheads wink with stars. And when they returned, with the crimson sunsets in their sails, it made a picture that pleased his eye. But it pleased him more, the handsome sum that his fleet would bring. And nothing, he said, would change his mind. Not even the priest who climbed the bluff to make his plea, bearing under his wide-brimmed hat a packet of pleas from all below. In the great hall of the lordly house the great man heard the words of the priest. He opened the packet and read to himself the topmost plea, then threw the rest into the fire that took the chill from the April morn.

"How long do they have?" the priest inquired.

The great one watched the packet of pleas go up in flame. "They have until the first of the week."

"Then God have mercy," the priest replied.

But the great man never went to church and didn't care what the priest replied. The state of his soul was much in doubt.

The priest bowed. "I shall pray for you and instruct my parish to pray for you."

"Pray away," said the great man. "I shall not change my mind for that. And in his face was the discontent that mocked his words and the lordly house . . . that had been ripening for years, like the wine he offered the good priest. For he owned a vineyard farther south. But the priest declined and went his way. He was very sad going down the bluff. He seemed to hurry with joyful news. It was all because of the steep incline. The village women watched him come and climbed the road a ways to him.

He shook his head. "I have failed," he said.

One of the women began to weep. "How shall the children be fed?" she asked.

"They shall eat the fish as they always have. We can fish for them at the end of the pier."

"And all the rest a child will need?"

Another woman spoke from the group. "We'll send Mara."

And another said, "If the father himself can't warm his heart, what earthly good can a little girl do?"

But the women agreed it was worth a try. What else was there? The priest agreed there was nothing to lose. The women urged him to teach the child the ways of prayer. He shook his head. "Why should I teach her the way to fail?" He left them and entered the church to pray.

So Mara was groomed for her mighty mission. Indeed, there was little time to lose. The women agreed on Easter Day. It was felt that God was especially open to Easter prayers and that the hardest of human hearts was softened ever so little then.

The men had left in the boats to fish. Perhaps it would be the final time, but no one knew. The word would come. The hour would strike. The women drew Mara into their midst. They told her as much as they knew to tell about the man and his fine house. Not one of them had been inside. They told her there would be people there, cousins of theirs, who would guide her up to the place to pray. And then they told her how to pray. They told her to ask the Holy Mother to soften the heart of the great man. Or if it were too much trouble to do, then simply to lead him to change his mind. For the purpose at hand an altered mind would serve as well as a softened heart. Though a softened heart was a safer thing. They told her that she must eat little supper and say her prayers when she went to bed at an early hour, and when she arose she must say her prayers, drink only water, eat no food, and leave without a word to say. Along the way she must think of nothing but God and the angels and speak to no one as she went.

Mara, brought in from a game of tag, listened to them with eyes

that could warm the heart of a stone and nodded her head with
its cloud of hair. She hoped she would not have to do it all, especially the part about no food. Her stomach ached to think of it.
And besides, she knew that praying was best when she wasn't
hungry.

For supper they brought her a slice of bread smeared with ever
so little butter. They gave her to drink a glass of plum juice mixed
with water the priest had blessed. They brushed her hair and put
her to bed and reminded her to say her prayers. But Mara was too
hungry to pray or even sleep. She lay in the twilight counting the
knotholes in the wall, hearing the children still at play, the cries
of birds, and the sound of waves as the tide came in. And when it
was too dark to see, she slipped barefooted into the pantry and got
herself some bread to eat.

When morning came they returned for her, signing her to
speak no words. They brushed her hair and braided it so tightly she
couldn't wrinkle her nose. They clothed her in her Sunday dress.
A blue jumper and snowy white embroidered blouse, whose
ruffles always tickled her chin. Her Sunday best was to gladden the
eye of the great man in case he happened to look her way. Her
prayers, they said, would gladden the Lord. But her best apparel
would gladden him too when worn to honor him Easter Day.

Long before the church bells rang, little Mara was on her way.
She had passed the pantry unobserved and filled one pocket with
chunks of bread. Then she passed the hutch where the rabbits lived
and slipped her favorite into her other jumper pocket. His name
was Frailie. She loved him dearly. She whispered to him to be very
still, and indeed he was. He understood. It made her happy to feel
his warmth against her side, to feel his softness with her hand. She
passed the church. The priest came out of his house nearby and
placed his hand upon her head. He signed her forehead with the
cross. He blessed her journey. He feared she would fail as he had

done. He knew the Lord has wonderful ways, but he could not believe in this as one.

At a little distance the women followed. Whenever she turned they waved to her. Some of them had the babies along. One was the boy who had breathed for Mara. He tugged at his mother and wanted to follow.

The men were at home and sick at heart. They were like the priest. They knew the Lord has wonderful ways . . . , but a little girl? Why not a boy? Why not the boy who lights the candles? Or the fine young lad who bears the cross?

Even Mara's father, who loved her dearly, could not but believe that his daughter would wear out her shoes for nothing. And then how was he to buy her more?

Mara took the road around the bluff, which gently wound and wound to the crest. It was not as hard as the one straight up. The April morning was chilly but fine. Mara trudged on and ate her bread. She shared some crumbs of it with a bird who crossed her path and twittered at her from a clump of flowers, small and pink. She sat on a rock among some ferns and took Frailie out to let him nibble the tips of them. And while he nibbled she finished her bread. When she chewed, the ruffles tickled her chin. So she loosened the tie of her pretty blouse and rolled them under and that was that. She picked up Frailie and kissed his ears and gave him the pocket with all the crumbs. She skipped along in the soft weeds beside the road, singing him songs, not Easter hymns but songs that a rabbit would like to hear. She made them up as she went along.

When she came to a stream with a little bridge, she left the bridge for somebody else. She took off the slippers her mother had polished to a shine and the clean white stockings her mother had washed and put them into her jumper pocket, and then she waded across the stream. The water, she thought, was deliciously cold. The hem of her jumper got wet, of course. Even Frailie was slightly damp. She sat on the bank to let him dry. There were friendly brown and white cows on the bank, who saw her there but didn't mind. They munched the grass and tinkled their bells. "How would you like that, Frailie?" she said. "To have a bell around your neck and make a song whenever you hopped?" She picked Frailie up and hopped with him, singing a bell song in his ear. She didn't put on her stockings and shoes until she reached the top of the bluff.

But once there, she sat on the ground and looked at the house, the largest she had ever seen. There were gardens around it with flowers just beginning to bloom and flowering trees already in bloom. She rubbed her feet in the soft grass, and then she put on her stockings and shoes. She found she was already hungry again. She heard the church bells far below. "Now be very still," she said to Frailie.

She discovered a door and knocked on it. A boy with a green cap answered it. When he saw her his mouth fell open. Presently he motioned her in and gently pushed her into a corner and hid her behind an array of aprons and woolen shawls. She reached for Frailie and held his ears.

Then the boy was back with an aproned woman, who chided him for hiding her. "Who's to notice her?" she said. "A tiny little thing like that." And she bent herself with a creaking of bones to plant a kiss on Mara's cheek. She was very plump and her white apron came all the way down to her fat feet spilling over her shoes.

She took Mara promptly by the hand and led her to the door of a great kitchen with pots and ladles that hung from the ceiling. Mara stood in the burst of hot, moist air and saw men and women like storybook people, so long were their aprons, so pink were their faces — some of them she had seen in the village — and smelled the most delicious of smells. Never before had she smelled such food. Tables were littered with hams and fowl cooked to a golden orange brown, and dishes of this and dishes of that. Another table held pies and tarts. The woman snatched up a flaky tart and gave it to Mara, who could not wait but ate it at once. It had a wonderful orangey taste.

"Poor little thing," the woman said, "she's hungry, and why shouldn't she be with all that climb? Did you have your breakfast, or did they make you leave it off?"

Mara didn't know how to answer. She simply stood and looked at the tarts. The woman gave her another one, spicy and warm with an apple taste. And then she opened a big soft bun and popped a slice of ham inside. "Take it along," the woman whispered. She gave her a napkin to wrap it in, and Mara put it into her pocket. A bowl of salad was by the door. "Could I have a little carrot?" she asked.

"That you can," and the woman daintily plucked one out with two plump fingers and dropped it into Mara's hand, who dropped it into the Frailie pocket.

By now the staff was pointing her out and smiling slyly. They seemed to know just why she was there. They seemed to be even more sure than Mara. Three of them kissed her on the cheek, and a large man with a red face, and under his apron a stomach as large as a large melon, slipped a hot pastry on top of Frailie, who shuddered and wiggled it off his ears.

Then the woman drew her back into the dusk of the hall and pointed to a steep flight of stairs at the end. "I'm going to put you in a little room. You're not afraid of the dark, are you?" She bent to Mara and whispered the words, while she held Mara's face in her floury hands. "You'll have to stay here and wait a while. He has to finish his Easter dinner. And then he'll come into the room next door where he meets a man about the boats. They're going to sign all the papers there. . . . Oh, me," she sighed, releasing Mara. She wiped her eyes with the edge of her apron and a dust of flour fell out of its folds. "You're so little. . . ."

Mara stood as tall as she could. She could feel Frailie at work on the carrot. In a moment the flour had made her sneeze.

"I hope you're not catching a cold," said the woman. "Do you think you can do it?"

Mara looked at her, wondering. "Do what?" she said.

"Why, pray him out of selling the boats."

Again, Mara didn't know how to reply. Before she prayed, she never thought. It was much like eating. She ate when hungry. She prayed when she wanted. Although they had said how much they wanted it, she didn't know yet how much she did. If the boats were sold, she thought it couldn't be half so bad as a baby sick or trying to breathe. The fathers would then be home all day and so could play with their children more. There would still be shells on the beach to find. There would still be games for them all to play and rabbits and kittens and dogs to love. There would still be mothers and fathers and friends.

The woman sighed and mopped her glistening face with her apron. "My nephew will lose his boat," she said. Mara glimpsed the hem of her raggedy dress and wondered if this was her Easter best.

Then the woman lifted her apron high, so as not to trip, and led Mara up the vertical stairs, as hard to climb as the bluff below. Behind the stairs the boy with the green cap stood and watched with eyes as shiny black as a trout. At the top the woman was out of breath. She put her fingers on her lips and hustled Mara down a hall and up another flight of stairs. Each step was laid with a carpet of green softer than seaweed fresh from the sea. Although it was noon, along the wall and in the shadowy curtained rooms lamps were glowing like fireflies.

The woman opened a narrow door and thrust the child into a room. She entered as well. Before the door was thoroughly shut

Mara saw the tiny room. Not much bigger than a closet, she thought. Indeed it seemed to be a closet. On the walls were shelves with blankets and sheets. One held baskets filled with all shapes and sizes of things. When the door was shut it was very dark. Mara held tight the ears of Frailie. The woman reached for Mara's head and patted it till they both grew accustomed to the dark. She tiptoed to the farthest wall and pushed aside a little board not very far above the floor. A shaft of light came streaming in. Mara could see the motes in it, drifting around like tiny bugs. The woman took Mara by the hand and drew her down and into the shaft and gently pushed her face to the wall.

Now that she knelt, Mara was seeing another room. It was very fine, with a large desk and shelves of books, a globe of the world, maps on the walls, all manner of ledgers and metal boxes. The carpet looked soft, a silvery gray with silver moons. Under the window was a narrow bed. There were pillows colored white and gold and a blue coverlet shot with gold. It was pretty enough for a lady's dress. The globe, she thought, was much the best. Its stand was polished until it shone.

The woman gently drew her back. "You must wait a while till he eats his meal. There is naturally more to eat today." Then sensing little Mara's thought, "Oh, no," she said, "Not all you saw. He has some family he doesn't like. They eat a lot. But he never waits for them to stop. He comes in here and takes a nap, and then he sits at his desk and writes. Today a man will come in and talk. They will talk about the sale of the boats. And then . . . and then he will sell them off. He will sign a paper, and then it will be over for them. Them in the village." She touched her apron to her eyes. Again Mara saw her raggedy dress in the shaft of light.

The woman went to one of the shelves and lit a candle waiting there. She carefully replaced the board, covering up the shaft of light. Candle shadows danced on the shelves as if little mice were playing there. "You must be very quiet," she said. "He mustn't suspect that you are here. Whenever you want to look at him, be sure to blow out the candle first before you go and move the board. If you don't he'll be sure to see the light."

Then she pointed out the extra matches. "Holy Mother, be merciful, don't set the place on fire," she said. She looked at Mara doubtfully. Her face was pink in the candlelight. "Does your mother let you strike a match?"

"She lets me light the fire," said Mara.

The woman nodded and went away, shutting the door with the greatest care. "Holy Mother, help her," she said.

As soon as her footsteps died away, Mara took Frailie out of her pocket and straightened his ears, which were badly bent. He had eaten most of his small carrot. The pastry with him was rather a mess. Some of it was in his ear. Mara cleaned it out with a handkerchief her mother had pinned inside her blouse. She kissed him tenderly on the head and hummed a little song for him, one she knew he always liked. And then she got out the bun with the ham, because by now she was hungry again.

Frailie hopped about the room. The room was cool. Mara lay down on the bare floor and looked at the shadows the candle made, over the ceiling, across the wall. She smelled the wax. After all her climb she was soon asleep. Frailie was worn from having to stay so long in a pocket and getting hot pastry in his ear. He hunched himself into a ball and slept and woke and slept and woke and slept. Rabbits never sleep for long. Being small and fashioned for peace and at the mercy of warlike things, they are born with a habit of taking care.

Mara was wakened by someone moving about next door. She heard the sound of a foghorn. But then she knew it was only a yawn. She got up and blew out the flickering flame. She crept on her hands and knees to the wall and ever so carefully moved the board. She could see a man stretched out on the bed. The beautiful cover was swept aside, and he lay on a blanket gray like the floor. His shining boots, straight and brown, watched like dogs beside the bed. He was not very tall, not nearly as tall as a man who owned so many boats should be. He had dark hair and a beard so black it was frightening. It was trimmed to a point but full and fierce. She stared until she was used to his beard. And after a bit, when he turned on his side, he looked to her helpless in his sleep.

She quietly took off her stockings and shoes. She sat on the floor with her legs crossed and her jumper tucked up under her feet. Frailie hopped into her lap. She cradled him and stroked his back. The man on the bed was moving his lips. A sorrowful look came into his face. It seemed to her that in his sleep the sadness spread to his arms and chest and over him to his very feet. The sadness of him came into her. He seemed as well like a little child, a little child to be held and rocked. She rocked Frailie and watched the man.

Suddenly he stirred and opened his eyes. He seemed to be looking straight into hers. His eyes were puzzled, as if he had been off somewhere and hadn't found his way home again. It was clear that he couldn't in fact see Mara sitting in darkness behind his wall, and yet it was clear that as he was looking where she sat, he was seeing darkly behind some wall inside himself. It seemed to Mara he had once had a little girl like herself, and now she was gone, Mara didn't know where. Mara sat and rocked them both, the sad child-man and the child of his. She kissed and kissed the ears of Frailie.

She heard a knock on the other door and a low woman's voice. "He waits below."

The man did not stir for ever so long. Then he sat up and put on his boots. He tossed away the handsome spread, then roughly whipped it over the bed, as fishermen smother a driftwood fire.

It was as if he stifled the flame of his life that slept. His face was no longer sad but weary. He opened a cabinet built into the wall and drew out a small decanter of wine and two crystal glasses finely etched. They gave a tiny tremulous cry when his weary fingers let them slip. Presently came another knock. He went to the door and opened it. And now in place of the weary look a smile of welcome crossed his face.

A taller man walked into the room. He too was smiling. His beard was white. There was not a hair on his shiny head. His eyes were blue and narrow as reeds, as if he knew things he didn't want his eyes to tell. The skin of his face told of the wind and sun and sea.

"Ah, Ramos," said the great one. "Have a glass of my special wine." And in his face was the discontent that had been ripening like the wine, that mocked the wine and the lordly house and the splendid sum he soon would make. Then his face relaxed into a smile. He poured the wine.

They sat and began to talk of the boats. They held their glasses up to the light and swirled the wine and sipped a bit. It was very fine to hear their talk. They threw their deep voices into it, as if they were calling across the water from boat to boat and back again, sounding hearty about it all, talking too about the wine, as if the sale were nothing at all, no more than sharing a glass of wine. As if the boats were paper ones they would launch for sport in a puddle of rain.

But underneath the great man's voice Mara was hearing something else. Something deep as a well in him. Or as if he were speaking down a well. And underneath his sociable look Mara was seeing his sleeping face when he was sad and his weary face when he awoke. His face for her was made of layers, like some of the shells along the shore, all of the faces there at once. The sad one was the plainest to her.

And because it was, she wanted to pray. She gathered herself up into herself. She had been told by the village women that she must pray to the Holy Mother. There were others, though, who said she should go to Jesus himself. Still others told her to pray to the saints. Amazing it is how people with small success at a thing will know precisely how it is done.

But Mara never did any of this. She went to God. He didn't sit on a throne in Heaven. He sat in a regular rocking chair. She had one at home that was much like his, but very much smaller than his, of course. She had only to think of her rocking chair. In her mind she would draw it up to his and, sitting beside him, begin to rock. Sometimes it would take a little while before her rocking was timed with his. But when it was, he would turn and smile a shining smile, as if he was glad to find her there and rocking exactly in time with him. God was very much taller than she and had today a delicious smell. As for that, it's possible Mara was smelling the pastry, the remains of which were in her pocket. But what did it matter? It didn't at all.

Mara rocked a little with Frailie. She whispered to God, "Good morning, God," as she always did, no matter what time of day it was. It was always morning when God was there, as if she had just got out of bed. She didn't have to ask a thing. He saw at once what the trouble was.

He said, "I'm glad you noticed it." And that was the way it always was. Perhaps it wasn't a prayer at all.

Always before, she had been quite close to what was amiss; holding the kitten, holding the baby's little hand. Now she was in another room. Nobody was sick or unable to breathe.

The great man was reading a sheet of paper. It was only a page, but it seemed to be taking him forever. The sociable look was on his face, but as he read she could tell it was somehow changing back to the weary look she had seen before and then from there to the sad face.

But Ramos did not notice this. Or if he did, he pretended he didn't. He twirled his glass and stared through the window. After a bit he raised the decanter beside his hand. "I'll help myself to a little more. Excellent sherry, most excellent. I congratulate you on bringing your vineyard to such a peak. Now that you're free of the fishing thing you'll concentrate on wine, I'm sure."

The great man didn't seem to hear. He went on reading. He appeared to have started over again. He read as if he were weary of it.

Mara kissed the ears of Frailie and rocked and rocked in time with God. And in her ears she was hearing bells. Strangely, not the chapel bells. They were like the cowbells on the slope. They too were ringing in time with God. Or it was God who made them ring in time with him.

"A problem?" Ramos said at last.

The great man silently shook his head.

"It pays to read it with care," said Ramos. "I recall a time when I gave the thing no more than a glance and found I'd signed away, well, more than I care to remember now." He chuckled and smiled into his wine. "I think you'll find no more written here than what we've both agreed upon."

The great man said, "Of course, of course." He told himself that his more than usual weariness grew out of thinking about the boats, what trouble they were, how many repairs they had to have, how much they cost to operate, and that as he read the document it followed he was reminded of this. He told himself that once he had signed the fleet away he would feel relief and a lift of the heart.

He drew the pen in its marble holder toward himself, but then he paused. In his mind was the clearest glimpse of his fishing vessels far out to sea, the sunlight glinting from stern and bow, the mastheads winking with little stars. He saw them again with the crimson sunset in their sails. It seemed to him he had never seen a finer sight. It occurred to him that his weariness rose not from the trouble of owning the boats but from having to think about their sale on a stomach full of an Easter meal, with a spirit laden with empty talk from relatives he didn't like. He resolved henceforth to eat alone. It seemed to him he was here now, and came here every day, in fact, to be rid of the sight and sound of them. That once he was here it followed that, in order to keep from going mad, he occupied himself. With what? The getting of money, the spending of it. As he sat here after his meal each day, with one hand he took it in and with the other he let it out. His head grew light to think of it. The sight of the boats was for every day, for the rest of his life if he wished it so. The handsome sum was a pleasure for once . . . until he let it out again.

But what is a pretty sight? He thought. On a misty day there's nothing there.

He picked up the pen, a quill he employed to take in money or let it out. He favored the way the ink ran full and dark with his name, almost as if it knew what he owned and how much more he was going to have. The quill was the blue of his coverlet. Mara saw the way he drew the tip of it under his chin behind the beard, a secret, very vulnerable place. She wanted to give him Frailie to hold. She thought how much it would comfort him, for now she felt his sadness rise, up, up inside his breast and farther up into his throat. Like the sea coming in at high tide, and when it came as far as it wished it let itself slide back again. But God, she felt, was holding it there, the sea that had always had its way, as the tide of his sorrow now was held. Only in sleep had his sorrow appeared. When he awoke he refused to see. This moment he saw how it claimed his shore. Higher and higher he saw it reach. Soon it would take his breath away.

She whispered to God, Don't let him be so very sad. But God was holding it just the same. And the great man now was seeing a sight he'd never bothered to see before. When the boats were in he would turn away. But now in the very heart of his mind he saw the men leap off the boats. He saw the women waving to them. He saw the children running to them. One child in particular caught his eye. A little girl, who stumbled and fell, but her father reached her and held her high, then caught her to him. She covered his face with a burst of hair. It might have been little Mara herself who ran and fell and was caught to him. Something about her recalled to his mind, the great man's mind, another child. Or perhaps, for the moment, to comfort and sadden, both at once, God had given him Mara to hold.

He dipped his pen in the ink to write. I could buy another fleet, he thought. There's nothing to say it shan't be so. I could buy a bigger and finer fleet. But the scene at the shore was in his mind, and he wished that nothing would ever change.

Tears stood in his eyes as he touched the tip of his pen to paper. And then there occurred an incredible thing. He could not at once recall his name. He remembered the name his mother had used and that one once dear had called him a name he had all but lost and now recalled but that was all.

He laid his quill pen gently down.

"There is a problem?" Ramos said, then extracted a watch to check the time.

The great man looked up in some surprise. "I find I have changed my mind," he said. He heard his words with astonishment.

And so it was the fleet was saved. The priest was sent back up the bluff with thankful letters under his hat. The great man didn't burn these up. He read them, every single one, and as he read his confusion grew. He stood for long at his seaward window.

And no one said, least of all the priest, that a great one's mercy will last forever. Like a stone in the brook mercy wears away. But the prayer of Mara is legend in the land.

The Flying Hawk

MISS EULALIA POTTS, librarian, was fond of dimming the lights, four times — three short dims and then a long, like the opening bars of Beethoven's Fifth. Fate knocking at the door, whatever. She wished to forewarn the heavy readers with a touch of tasteful severity that in twenty minutes she would cast them out. They would surface briefly, eyes drugged with words, and plunge back in like earthworms trying to avoid the light, but a corner of the mind had been dismayed, could make a decision to check things out, even recall where the card was kept. It was a smallish sort of town, but for thirty years Miss Potts had run as tight a ship as any urban librarian.

Just to the right of the checkout desk was a banner, framed, of needlepoint that proclaimed with a floral embellishment: "There is no frigate like a book." And to the left, a similar one that made its statement without adornment: "Silence is golden." Miss Potts herself had fashioned neither. She openly despised the needle. One sewed to escape from reading. But high above Miss Potts's head hung an unframed plea of modest size that she indeed had made herself: "When turning pages, please refrain from moistening the thumb." Children, of course, were in awe of Miss Potts and never outgrew their awe of her and passed it on to children of theirs. She liked the children. She secretly despised the heavy readers. They read to avoid the challenge of Life. They were failures.

When Caleb Dawkins came in just after she had dimmed the lights, she hoped he would not wander vaguely but state his business in a forthright way. He was not a child nor a heavy reader. She found that she could recall his name, though he almost never trod her turf. He would be in high school, she supposed, but of course his sweater was emblazoned with it, Class of '37.

He shuffled to her reluctantly. "Miss Potts, you got some books in here would help me write a history paper?"

"On what subject?"

"Any subject. For American History. I can't think of none."

"Are you given a list of possible subjects?" He shook his head in youthful mourning. "What period of American History?"

"She don't care."

"She couldn't possibly have turned you loose on the entire sweep of American History."

He looked away into the stacks. "She don't care."

"Doesn't care." She sighed. "Couldn't you have come in earlier?" But looking down at his grubby hands and weary eyes she saw that he must have been involved with something strenuously athletic. She studied him with speculation. And then she asked, "Are you strong and healthy?"

The question caused him some surprise.

"But of course you are if you're on the team. Unless the sweater belongs to your brother."

"No, ma'am," he said. "I'm on the team." He waited a moment. "About the paper, Miss Gibson says I have to have ten references. Three of them got to be magazines."

Miss Potts whooped. "Lila Gibson! I remember her with sticky hands. All over the books. They smelled of gum. She used a Tootsie Roll for a bookmark."

"Miss Gibson did? Wow!" he said.

"Blackmail her into a passing grade."

He did not quite know how to proceed. With most adults you could get some kind of a vague idea where the conversation was going to lead. Miss Potts was really different, though.

She looked at the clock above the desk. "It's closing time. I might have something in mind for you. Come back tomorrow afternoon."

He shifted his feet. "Ma'am, I got practice after school."

"Well, that doesn't last all afternoon. Get a shower and be here just as soon as you can."

"Yes, ma'am," he said.

As he turned to leave she pinioned him with a hushed, librarian's throaty call, lots of wind but not much voice: "Caleb, do you know how to drive a car?"

And now of course he was really amazed. "I can drive my uncle's truck," he said.

She smiled and dimmed the lights again. She was girding her loins to throw out the man with his head in the Sunday *Times* and the girl who slept with her face on a book.

CALEB WAS BACK the next afternoon. He had pondered the wisdom of not showing up, but he had to pass history to play on the team.

"Why are you limping?" she asked him sternly.

"I turned my foot in the practice game."

"Is it serious, then?"

"No, ma'am," he said.

"You'll need both feet by the time we're through."

Nothing she said to him made any sense. She led him back behind the desk and past the stacks of yellowing weeklies and under the stairs and into her lair. She had maps and pictures all over the walls, photographs that were brown with age, nothing that had any color to it, except for one that he knew from Miss Clifford's class. *The Birth of Venus.* He had missed who painted it on the test.

Miss Potts saw him looking at the tits of Venus. She all but snapped her fingers at him. "Sit down," she said. "Sit down, sit down. We don't have a lot of time to waste. Soak that foot in Epsom salts as soon as you get home tonight."

"Yes, ma'am," he said, and then he sat.

She sat as well, behind her desk. "American History you say it is? Well, Caleb, I have the thing for you. That is, of course, if you're quite in earnest. And steadfast too. Loyal to things you undertake."

He felt that she knew the Boy Scout oath, knew it by heart, might even ask him to say it to her. His foot was throbbing. "Yes, ma'am," he said.

She crossed her arms on the orange blotter and leaned toward him. "Above all, Caleb, a sense of daring. And a thirst for knowledge. Do you have it, Caleb?"

He stirred uneasily. "I reckon, ma'am."

She fixed him with a wintry eye. "What kind of answer is that?" she said. "Do you or don't you have a thirst?"

"Yes, ma'am, I do." He thought of sitting at Richardson's Drugs, having a Coke with the rest of the team.

She took a long deep breath at that. Her eyes just brushed the Venus rising out of the sea. She opened and shut the drawer of her desk. She scooped the pencils into a pile and pushed them to the edge of the blotter. She rested upon him her sad, firm gaze. "Are you acquainted with the facts of life?"

He felt his face grow slightly warm. "Ma'am? What facts?"

She folded her hands. "People who quibble always are. . . . Well, that's settled. I had to know. My function is not. . . . I cannot in conscience destroy an innocence. . . . Now," she began in a businesslike tone, "I want you to look at two photographs. They're on the wall. No, you'll have to get up. Do you see those two men under the map? The pictures are made from daguerreotypes."

Caleb got up and limped to the wall. One he was sure of. All that beard, it had to be. "I reckon it's Lincoln."

"Who is the other, would you say?"

He shook his head.

"Do they look alike?"

He stared at the men. "I reckon they do. Some, I guess."

"Some?"

"Well, a lot, I guess."

"And can you guess why that is?" she asked.

"Maybe because they're kinfolks, ma'am?"

"You have made a brilliant deduction, Caleb. You have taken the first exciting step. Research begins with such a step. All research. All research. . . . Are you wondering about the other man?"

He could tell from her tone that he had to wonder. "Yes, ma'am," he said.

"She left him to wonder a little while. "Jefferson Davis," she said at last. "Two mighty leaders locked in combat. Two presidents . . . two brothers, mortal enemies."

He continued to stand and stare at the face. He didn't know what else to do. One shoe was tight. His foot was beginning to swell a bit. He wanted to sit and undo the lace.

"You may well be stunned. As I was stunned."

"Yes, ma'am," he said.

"Sit down, Caleb. There is much to be done."

He could tell that her voice had a different tone. It occurred to him it was like the coach addressing the team before the game. The words were different. The tone was the same.

"Caleb, I propose to equip you with a revelation that if rightly imparted will change the course of history." She thought of this while she toyed with a pencil. "Let us say, instead, the interpretation of history. Or, rather, we should say the writing of history. Do you understand me, Caleb?"

"No, ma'am," he said.

"Well, presently you will. We shall start at the beginning. In the paper you will write for Miss Lila Gibson of the sticky fingers you will start at the beginning." She swirled her desk chair till the back of her head and a knob of gray hair was all he could see. Her hairpins stuck out like a porcupine's quills. Her finger skated along a row of green books behind her desk and extracted one. She half whirled back and opened it. He saw that she had a hairpin inside it to mark the place.

She swirled herself back to him all the way. "I shall read from the *Encyclopaedia Britannica*. There is no higher authority. Remember that, Caleb. And when you spell it for Lila Gibson, please spell it with an 'ae' instead of an 'e.'" She looked at him sternly.

"Yes, ma'am," he said.

She stared at him with abstracted eyes. "On second thought, I'm tempted to skip the beginning for now and plunge right in. Beginnings are inclined to be tedious." She seemed to require his confirmation.

"Yes, ma'am," he said.

"How old are you, Caleb?"

"Seventeen," he said. Well, he would be in a couple of months.

She listened with barely courteous distaste. "That's not very old, I'm afraid," she said. "However," she added with rising cheer, "time is in our favor."

"Yes, ma'am," he said.

"Coming of age is a moment in time." Her eyes skimmed Venus and dropped to the volume she held in her lap. Abruptly she snapped it shut on the hairpin. She opened her desk drawer and drew out a key with which she opened another drawer. From this second drawer she extracted a book, which she opened with the extremest care. Caleb saw it was ready to fall apart. It was more like a notebook than a book. It had small sheets of caramel-colored, square-cut paper dimly, closely written over with pen.

Miss Potts gently cleared her throat. "From time to time people favor us with gifts of books. They are cleaning house or moving away. Or people die, and after their relatives divide the spoils they give us anything that's left. Like *The Rover Boys*. We've thirteen sets. There's a box in the basement that's just come in. It will probably give us another set. I make it a policy to take it all. Some day they may give us something we want. Some gem they are totally unaware. . . ." A reminiscence curled her lip. "And that is how we came to possess this original copy of a diary written by a Mrs. Mary Gilpin, who wrote about her daily life in 1809 in rural Kentucky.

"Her spelling is poor." She glanced at him, as if somehow she had heard of his.

"Yes, ma'am," he said.

"I shall read from an entry dated February seventeenth of that year: 'This weak Nancy Lincoln was delivered of a boy. My feeling is it is not Toms boy. I told Sarah Hutton, her feeling is the same. Nancy tuk on work at The Flying Hawk ten months ago, a little more. She tuk her little girl along and lef her each day with the gardners wife who had too of her own. Sarah Hutton says Seth says their come a gentlemun from south of hear. Name of Davis he said with a fine blooded hoarse had throne a shoe. he was on his way from some manner a busyness in Louisville and headed home when his hoarse went lame. He was three nites their and Nancy went up to his chamber to clene and Seth says the rumor went that it tuk a blessed long time to clene. She worked on their for another 3 months and then she tuk sick and didnt go back and Ham Wesleys daughter tuk her place.'"

She looked up at him. "Caleb," she said, "are you following me?"

"Not exactly, ma'am."

She sighed and frowned. "What this is saying in the plainest English, however badly spelled, is that this woman Gilpin has reason to believe that a man named Davis fathered Abraham Lincoln. If this man in question was Samuel Davis, he was headed home to be with his wife before she delivered on June the third his tenth and last child named Jefferson. And he stopped at the inn where Nancy, the mother of Lincoln, worked. Except that she wasn't the mother of Lincoln, but she would be in another nine months. I have utterly no use for such a man! I wish to put it in the strongest terms."

Caleb looked bewildered.

Miss Potts rolled her eyes and turned them away. "History is full of these peccadilloes. I wouldn't besmirch your ears with it, except that embedded in this miserable oyster is the rarest of pearls. I refer to the cause of the Civil War."

"Ma'am, Miss Gibson said we shouldn't get into causes or nothin'."

"Bother, Miss Gibson! A girl who would mark her place with a Tootsie Roll, unwrapped at that! We shall just have to get around Miss Gibson, throw her a Tootsie Roll to gnaw. Our goal is Grand Prize in the statewide History Competition, and after that, Caleb, your future is made. She must not be allowed to blight your future."

"Ma'am, this paper was just for Miss Gibson."

"We must set our goal higher than Lila Gibson. I have the address."

He decided that she was just as batty as any bedbug could possibly be, but most adults seemed to be slightly off. And he recalled that he had to pass history or else he couldn't play on the team.

She smiled in a way that slapped a claim on him — like maybe she was kin or something like that — and shoved her hairpins into her knob. Her bright eyes took in the photographs, climbed to Venus, then veered and plummeted to the map. "Caleb," she said, "you do understand that a diary, however revealing it seems, will lack the punch of *Britannica*? By punch I mean authority. But facts observed, recorded, Caleb, by eye and ear. . . . Observation of fact is the mother of history. So, Caleb, what I propose to you is a prudent trip to the scene of the action."

He hadn't an idea what she meant. "A trip to where?" he finally asked.

"To The Flying Hawk, wherever else?"

"Ma'am, I missed that part about the bird."

Her look was withering. "The Flying Hawk is the name of the inn where the fate of the South began to be born."

"I thought you said it was Abraham Lincoln."

"But Lincoln, Caleb, started the war. And all for envy. All for envy. Envy is one of the Deadly Sins."

"Yes, ma'am," he said.

"We'll discuss Envy along the way. Do you think you could get your uncle's truck and pick me up next Saturday?"

"Ma'am?" he said. He was utterly amazed.

"I thought you told me you knew how to drive your uncle's truck."

"That don't mean he's gonna let me take it."

"He will," she said. "I'll write him a note. I'll mention Miss Gibson." She smiled at him with a trace of glee. "I can always mention that atlas he borrowed and left in the rain. Before your day. Argentina was washed away. A total loss."

Right on the spot she wrote the note. "And Caleb, be sure to bring a shovel and pick."

He could only stare.

"In case," she said, "it comes to that. Well, it isn't a matter of digging for Troy."

HE WAS SURE his uncle would save his skin. Tell him he couldn't have the truck. For by now he thought he'd rather flunk history than ride off down the road with old lady Potts and a shovel and pick, leave Tennessee and cross into Kentucky where he didn't belong and neither did she. Ordinarily he was eager to drive whenever his uncle would give him the chance. His uncle suspected him of racing the truck and put him off most of the times he asked. But to his entire dumbfounded amazement his uncle embraced the whole idea, thought that maybe his grade would improve enough that he could stay on the team. And he trusted Miss Potts to keep him from racing. But just in case she lost control, he had a governor put on the truck, which would keep them from racing over thirty-five.

It was early May and the sky was fair, with only a wisp of fog in the trees. Miss Potts had said to leave at seven. She was waiting for him in front of her house, which was covered with vines. Her whole front yard was covered with bricks, but grass and a lot of stuff leaked up. She climbed up into the cab with him. He had never seen her dressed up before. Clearly it wasn't in her plan to use the pick or the shovel herself. Her black and white dress was printed with sprays of . . . it looked like oats. A black felt hat was pushed over her brow to make a space for her knot at the back. She carried a purse that was speckled with beads, a lemon-colored hamper of straw, which she said contained their picnic lunch, and two umbrellas, one for each of them. He hoped nobody would see them leave.

Once inside, she took off her hat. "This is going to be an adventure, Caleb. I feel it all the way down to my toes. Mind and body and spirit, Caleb. Each in turn and all at once."

"Yes, ma'am," he said.

"May is the finest month for travel." She had maps with the lunch in her big straw hamper, and she got them out and spread them about all over the cab till he couldn't see to shift the gears. In a voice of elation she ordered, "Head north. You notice," she said, "I'm not whispering. I'm obliged to whisper all week long. Can't you go a little faster?" she asked.

"No, ma'am, I can't. My uncle has done put a governor on it."

"Can't you take it off?"

"No, ma'am, he'd skin me alive if I did."

"Well, he won't skin me. Nobody skins a librarian. Pull over to the side. Do you have some tools?"

He couldn't believe it. She selected a screwdriver, pliers, and wrench and went in under the hood like a pro. He was in a sweat that somebody who knew him would come along. He slumped in the seat. When she climbed back in, she confided with glee, "I never could stand something holding me back."

"Yes, ma'am," he said. He couldn't say why, but he thought of Venus and her naked tits.

He was really relieved when they crossed the border. The chances were better that they wouldn't run into somebody he knew. The sun was bright. The air was soft and smelled of summer. The land was green. The pick and shovel made a rat-tat-tat in the bed of the truck. She invited him to join her in singing "My Old Kentucky Home," but he couldn't bring himself to that. He listened to her while she belted it out like the coach on the day before a game. "I enjoy not having to whisper," she said. "I let it all out the entire weekend."

"Yes, ma'am," he said. She sounded to him a little crocked.

With the governor off, they made good time. He didn't know what they were looking for, unless it could be that hawk location.

"You find that place on the map you got, ma'am?"

She laughed aloud. "Of course not, Caleb. That inn was a century and a quarter ago. I don't expect to find it there. There might be a stone or two left on the spot. We might have to shovel a little dirt. If it's still there, it will be something else. We might have to jimmy a lock or two. We shall certainly do some detective work. Are you familiar with Sherlock Holmes?"

"No, ma'am," he said. "Is he somebody we're lookin' for?"

She gave a snort. "You don't appear to be much of a reader."

"No, ma'am," he said.

"A pity," she said. "When you come to writing this essay of yours, all you've read will be food for it."

"Yes, ma'am," he said. With the mention of food he was suddenly hungry. He eyed the hamper she kept on the floor between her feet. There wasn't a lot of room in the cab. From time to time she spread her map all over the gears.

In a couple of hours she announced they were there.

He honestly didn't know where that was. She made him pull off the road a ways and showed him the tiny dot on the map. "That's where the Lincolns were married, Caleb, and where they were living when little Abraham was conceived. And here we're only a few miles away. Thomas was a drifter, by all accounts, and a poor provider. So Nancy got some work at the inn and walked to it carrying her little girl. It must be somewhere close to here. And what we have to do, of course, is comb this region to find some traces of the inn. A building stone or two will do. Some tumbled piles of weathered bricks. In winter each guest would have had a fire. A structure on the verge of collapse would be a promising sign, I think."

He couldn't believe they had come this far, over eighty miles, and this was all she knew to say. He looked at the countryside dotted with trees and a few lone houses. "Ma'am, you think we should ask in town?"

"You think I haven't thought of that? I have already written the Chamber of Commerce. As a matter of fact, some time ago. They claim no knowledge of The Flying Hawk Inn. And it doesn't surprise me in the least. Not in the least. Not in the least."

He couldn't think why it didn't surprise her. It surprised him a lot. And then it didn't surprise him a bit.

"Caleb." She patted him on the arm. "I think you'll find me a homing pigeon. I have an instinct for finding things, which is strongly developed by my profession. It's taken me years, but I say it now with all modesty: I am able to locate any book misshelved by a careless or malicious hand. I home right in on that little lost book."

"Yes, ma'am," he said, "but I'm too hungry to drive any more."

"It's early," she said, "but I honor the need. Pull under that tree."

While he stuffed his mouth with chunks of fried chicken and hardboiled eggs and washed them down with warm lemonade, she sat in the weeds and read to him out of the *Britannica*, a volume of which had emerged from the hamper along with the lunch. Below the hem of her dress imprinted with all the oats — across the road he could see a field of them barely up — her pink slip boldly proclaimed itself. She seemed to regard him as some sort of kin she wouldn't mind seeing her underwear. He looked away from it into the trees. He wished to be anywhere else in the world.

Between tiny bites of her egg salad sandwich she explained to him that Nancy Hanks was a natural child. "That means her father didn't marry her mother. I have utterly no use for such a man!" She looked at him with severity, as if she suspected he harbored the seeds. With a little shock, he saw her reach into the neck of her dress and toss the oats and pull some glasses out of her breast, or whatever was in there behind the oats. She settled the glasses on and read: "'Nothing is known of the father of Nancy Hanks, though there is a persistent tradition that he was a Virginia aristocrat.' Note that, Caleb. I find it of grave significance." She resumed her reading. "'Nancy's famous son appears to have believed the story and to have felt that whatever distinction he possessed had come from this unacknowledged heritage of aristocracy.' Note that, Caleb. This champion, as we see him, of the common man, and all the time he yearns for the gentry who rejected his mother."

She dragged another book from the hamper and found the hairpin that marked the place. "Carl Sandburg has written the definitive life. Your paper must give him a footnote or two. According to Sandburg, her mother would croon in the evening to Nancy, 'Hush thee, hush thee, thy father's a gentleman.' Note, Caleb, that at the earliest age there is planted in Nancy a knowledge that the life which is rightfully hers she has been denied from the moment of birth. Life on a Virginia plantation, Caleb, faithful darkies to do her bidding, splendid balls, dazzling gowns, highborn admirers. As she grew older, imagine, Caleb, the rebellion stirring in her breast."

He thought of Venus.

She noted that his attention strayed. "You are asking, Caleb, how Sandburg knew what the mother would croon. I can only say that a man of research will come to a knowledge of fact through his pores, perhaps as I come to the misshelved book. Which is not to say that you and I will rely on our pores. We must rely on a pick and shovel."

She snaked her glasses down through the oats and into her chest. She gathered things up and into her hamper. She got to her feet with a richer display of her slip than ever. "Well, onward and upward! The grass will be growing under our feet."

He struggled up. His foot was asleep. "Which way, ma'am?"

She pointed gaily down the road. "Drive till I tell you to stop," she said.

The only thing left to do was drive. The grownups had really enslaved the young, but Lincoln had never bothered with that. You didn't get power until you were old, and then you forgot what kids went through. He blamed his uncle for most of this. He always said no when you needed yes. When you needed no, he couldn't wait to come up with yes. They were whipping along at a fast little clip over bad dirt roads. The truck was bouncing and rattling its fenders. The pick and shovel were thumping and clashing away in the rear. The dust was flying, when all of a sudden Miss Potts cried, "Stop!"

They were passing a little house back from the road. She ordered him firmly to hop a ditch and drive up close. When he did, the hounds came from under a bush and jumped all over the side of the truck.

Miss Potts's lips were set in a smile, as if she enjoyed a good barking at. After about five minutes of this, a woman came around the side of the house and told the dogs they had better shut up. Miss Potts leaned out and called to her sweetly in a voice pitched up from her library voice and down a peg from "Old Kentucky Home." "You look as if you know this region quite well. Would you happen to know the whereabouts of an old, old inn called The Flying Hawk?"

The woman pushed the hair up out of her face and held it there like the brim of a hat and simply stared.

"Think hard, my dear," said Miss Potts with patience. "I'm very anxious to find that inn or even the place where it used to be. An inn is something like a small hotel. I'm very sure it was close to here."

The dogs whined in a lonesome way. The woman came to some sort of life. She dropped her hair and pointed her finger. "You go on down to the next house down. Yella house sits back from the road. Real old man, he sits in the yard. He might could tell you. He's ninety-eight."

"Thank you, my dear. I'm indebted to you." And Caleb saw Miss Potts blow her a kiss. He felt that things were coming unglued and would only get worse. He was sure of it.

Sure enough, the old man was out in the yard. His chair was under a sweet gum tree. A breeze was ruffling his snow white hair. Miss Potts was really excited to see him. "I told you, Caleb, I have an instinct. There sits the book that has been misshelved. The scholars have all of them passed him by because when they happened to come along he was sitting here and not on the shelf. I venture to say that before we're done we shall bring the *Britannica* to its knees."

Miss Potts was aware of the proper course. She marched to the door of the yellow house with its crumbling brick pillars and its dogs sleeping under the sagging porch and its sociable speckled hens in a huddle. She knocked while Caleb sat in the cab. With reluctant eyes, he watched her conversing at length with the screen. She turned around and waved him out. "Permission is granted," she cheerily called. And when he approached, "Anyone that's as old as this, you have to check with the owner first."

"Somebody owns him?" Caleb asked.

"Of course," she said. "His granddaughter does."

"Miss Gibson says the Civil War was fought for that."

"Lila Gibson knows nothing at all. Your paper will tell her why it was fought."

All the time the old man was sitting nearby as if he wasn't aware of them.

"His granddaughter says he is very deaf. You may have to lend me your voice for this."

Caleb hoped it wouldn't come to that. He hoped that when he

was ninety-eight . . . but happily Miss Potts would be dead by then, with Abraham Lincoln and all the rest. He stationed himself behind the tree, to blend with the branches as best he could. Miss Potts had sailed right up to the man and plopped herself into a chair at his side. She even knew his name, it seemed.

"Mr. Putney," she yelled, "I'm Eulalia Potts. I'm trying to find The Flying Hawk."

He turned his head very slowly to her. The breeze was tumbling and tossing his hair.

"The Flying Hawk. Have you heard of it?"

He waved his hand slowly in front of his face, as if he was batting a fly away.

"The Flying Hawk. You remember it?"

He spoke to the air in a quavering voice. "Flies is bad."

"The Flying Hawk." She had pitched her yell to a higher key. "Tell me about The Flying Hawk."

Caleb could see there wasn't much of him left, and Miss Potts was going to wipe out that. There wouldn't be enough to scrape off the grass. He was in worse shape than the diary book that had started all this, but she didn't care how she handled *him*. He tried to sneak off and get in the cab. But Miss Potts spied him and beckoned him over. "Repeat these words as loud as you can: 'Do you remember The Flying Hawk?'"

He saw that the sooner he did what she said, the sooner they could get in the truck and leave. So he walked up close and yelled to the pink and hairy ear, "Do you remember The Flying Hawk?"

"The Flyin' Hawk? A course I do."

Caleb nearly fell over him. The man had a weak, breathy, trembly voice, as if he were riding a bumpy road and the motion had got him tuckered out.

Eulalia Potts had stars in her eyes. "Tell us what you recall," she shrieked into his ear.

He looked at her, puzzled, and shook his head.

At that moment a woman with bouncy blonde hair and her arm in a sling came out of the house. With her one good arm she carried a tray with a pitcher of something and glasses for all. She laid it down on the grass at their feet. From the smell Caleb knew it was lemonade. A sociable hen walked over to look and to have a peck at Miss Potts's oats. The woman shooed it away with her foot. She drew from her apron some gold-rimmed glasses. They belonged to the man, for she slipped the ear pieces over his ears, one at a time because of her arm. Then she drew from her apron a large black object in the shape of a horn, which she handed with a tight little smile to Miss Potts.

"I guarantee this here is the best." She spoke in a strained, librarian's whisper. "My voice box is done gone down the drain."

"Well, well," said Miss Potts, caressing the trumpet, "you're as welcome as spring. And Caleb, you help this good woman, you hear, with whatever she's brought to refresh our day. I see that you've injured your arm, my dear."

"It takes it outa the bones, you know. You yell the stiffenin' outa your bones."

"That's an interesting fact," Miss Potts observed.

Caleb poured lemonade and passed it around. The old man spilled half of his down his front. But his granddaughter pulled a towel from her apron and mopped him off.

Miss Potts boomed her questions into the trumpet, which she held to his ear. "Is The Flying Hawk still standing today?"

He shook his head.

"Do you know where it is?"

He pointed due north, but his finger shook itself into northeast, then veered again to east southeast. Caleb, sipping his drink, felt a great relief. Since he couldn't be asked to circle the compass, he would probably not have to dig at all. But he couldn't of course be sure of it.

Miss Potts was undaunted. "Tell me what you have heard of it."

He snuffled some lemonade up his nose and fell to sneezing. His teeth flew out, but his granddaughter clapped them back into place. He closed his eyes. "Seem like I fell in the pond," he said. "I reckon somebody fish me out."

Miss Potts pursued him. "The Flying Hawk!"

His eyes were still shut. "It's kinda slippery. I'm tryin' to find a place I cin hold. Gotta find a place to keep from slippin'."

"He don't mean the pond," his granddaughter said. "He's afflicted with slippery recollection."

"Indeed," said Miss Potts, "it afflicts us all."

"He's got a mind in a delicate way. Jus' leave 'im be for a little spell."

But he opened his eyes and looked around. "Day I uz twelve year ol', see, my granpappy he live . . . he live . . . he live . . . well, I fergit."

He slapped at the trumpet, which tickled his ear. He lapsed into silence.

"Go on," yelled Miss Potts.

"He come and he he'p me shoe my fust hoss. It uz the fust hoss I ever shoed. Didn't do too good." He showed them his teeth in a silent laugh. "He uz tellin' as how he used to shoe hosses fer The Flyin' Hawk and how he done twelve hosses one day. He tol' me . . . tol' me . . . toll me he shoed his fust un' at twelve, jus' like I done my fust at twelve. He tol' me that. Day I uz twelve." The old man seemed to be pleased with his tale.

Miss Potts raised the trumpet again to his ear. "Did he speak of the people who stayed at the inn? Any one at all?"

He shook his head and slapped at the horn.

But she restored it. "Think hard," she yelled.

"He don't like to think," his granddaughter said. "It makes him itch."

"Nobody likes to think," said Miss Potts, booming into his horn. "But as long as we're alive we have to think."

Two retrievers and three speckled hens had raised their heads. The old man scratched and shook his own.

"Mr. Putney," bellowed Miss Potts again, "do you . . . are you a God-fearing man?"

He swayed a little. His granddaughter said, with modest pride, "He knows about ever' hymn there is."

"The good Lord put you here to think."

He scratched his chest.

"That means he's thinkin'," the woman said.

"Caleb," said Miss Potts in the grimmest of tones. "I think this calls for extravagant measures. Bring me my hamper out of the truck."

He didn't think the old man could take any more, for he guessed that her plan was to holler *Britannica* stuff aloud. He thought it would finish the old man off. Caleb had barely survived it himself, at a reasonable pitch. But he fetched the hamper and dropped it with sorry grace at her feet. And then to his everlasting shock she pulled from its depths a bottle of whiskey. In a Nu-Grape bottle but whiskey, all right. She lifted the old man's lemonade glass that had slid to the ground and poured into it a portion of spirits. She turned to the woman. "This is wholesome spirits made of wholesome corn. I carry it for a medicinal need. With your permission. . . ."

The woman looked doubtful. "Well, he ain't sick. Old ain't sick."

"Of course he's sick. He refuses to think. Spirits will restore his brain to its function."

The granddaughter frowned, but her hair couldn't keep itself out of a bounce that signaled yes. "He's liable to start singin' all them hymns."

"We'll take the risk," Miss Potts replied. She poured a drop of it into the trumpet and tipped the rest of it into his mouth. He swallowed and coughed a little and smiled. He began to scratch.

Miss Potts leaned over and gave him a nice little pat on the arm. "Now, think," she roared.

A couple of crows cawed over their heads and perched on the shovel and pick in the truck. The old man watched them and scratched and smiled. "Put me . . . put me in mind a my pappy. Said he carried a pick. He uz diggin' fer gold."

"No, no," said Miss Potts. "The Flying Hawk."

"He uz diggin' away an' there come up a rattler rattlin' away . . ."

"Whisky can get him switched off the track," the woman observed with a bob of her hair. "Someone that's old, they is delicate made."

"Caleb, hide the shovel and pick in the cab. My good woman, you seem to be full of invention."

Caleb went off to do as told. The granddaughter took the horn from Miss Potts, and holding it, hollered into his ear, with astonishing violence in view of her previous absence of vigor. The hens scattered. The crows took flight. It sounded to Caleb like "Cannon ball!" "It shakes him outa wherever he's at."

"I assume he saw action in the War," said Miss Potts.

It seemed to work, for he slipped back into The Flying Hawk as if he had never strayed from it. He nodded his head. "I recollec' he said . . . he said . . . he said there was a gentleman from south a here had a fine-blooded hoss had thowed a shoe. Finest hoss he ever seed. He shoed his hoss an' the gentleman give 'im a piece a silver . . . Ain't money . . . ain't money . . . ain't money. . . ."

The old man clearly suffered a need to prime his speech with a couple of words, and then he threatened to stick on them. "Give 'im a leetle hoss done made a silver. He tol' me . . . he tol' me . . . he tol' me he kep' it all them . . . all them years an' carried it with 'im to bring 'im luck. He said it done it. It brung 'im luck. Ain't nothin' better'n luck, by God." He flashed his gums. "He showed it me. It shore was purty. Had leetle hoofs an' all, it did. He give it 'cause he said . . . he said . . . he said . . ."

He seemed to stick. Miss Potts leaned forward and thumped him lightly. He went straight on. "My granpappy put 'im in mind a his boy back home uz mighty nigh twelve as same as him, an' he said . . . he said . . . he had another un' good as borned, an' he uz aimin' to make it home afore it come, an' that uz why he needed that hoss as bad as he done . . . an' that uz why . . . that uz why he give my granpappy done the shoein' that leetle hoss had hoofs an' all."

Miss Potts fairly trumpeted into his horn. "What was the name? The name of the man?"

He scratched his stomach and shook his head, and suddenly he fell asleep.

"Was the name Davis?" Miss Potts was hoarse. But he slept with a peaceful smile on his face. "Could we have the 'Cannon ball' once more?"

But his granddaughter firmly flung her locks. "When he goes to sleep, ain't nothin' you can say. Dynamite won't bring 'im back."

Miss Potts fell back in her chair quite limp. "I do believe I have yelled the stiffening out of my bones." She poured some whiskey down her throat. "A medicinal need," she croaked to Caleb.

"Yes, ma'am," he said.

She poured some more and corked the bottle. She restored it to her hamper and rose. Whatever else, she had yelled the hairpins out of her hair. Caleb thought the back of her looked like a windmill.

"This has been a physical encounter indeed," she told them brightly, clearing her throat again and again. "Caleb, be good enough to put the hamper back in the truck. Madam, I thank you for the lemonade and for the use of your interesting kin, who I'm sure is very dear to you. We have primed the pump, yes, primed the pump. He may recall something later on, and here is my card. I'd be much obliged if you'd get in touch." She rummaged around in her beaded purse and found a card. "If the names of Davis or Nancy surface, we'll return for a glass of your fine lemonade."

Caleb heard it and set his jaw. He told himself that nothing that even came close to this was ever . . . ever . . . ever (he found that he was stuck on the word and maybe this trip had turned him old) . . . about to suck him in again.

He couldn't get out of there fast enough. His tires spit dust. He found a store down the road that sold gas. Miss Potts didn't offer to pay for any. He guessed this trip was supposed to be his. She was pulling the *Britannica* out of her hamper to read to him in a rusty voice. "A 'forest madonna,' they have called her, Caleb. I am reading, Caleb. 'Good-looking, sensitive, pious, with an air that seemed to bespeak a different social world from the one in which she moved.' You could improve on the language here. I have utterly no use for the word 'bespeak.' She was also something of a dreamer, it says. I suppose you couldn't take notes and drive."

"No, ma'am," he said.

She suddenly clapped the volume shut. "We may have occasion to write the *Britannica*." She pulled out Sandburg, knocking the gears. "He calls her shrewd and dark and lonesome. She was 'shaken with sacred desires,' he says. Caleb, my boy, you have yet to learn, when it comes to desire, how close the sacred and profane can be, how swiftly one can turn into the other."

Miss Potts's voice was low and husky. He guessed it was from the shouting she'd done. But maybe the whiskey was part of it, for he smelled it strong in the air of the cab. She sounded the way they did in the movies. "She is drawn to this gentleman from the south with all his land and his blooded horses. Her superior lineage is drawn to his. And he sees in her . . . a forest madonna but something more. No woman like this has ever cleaned a chamber of his before. She was there for him. That day he took her."

"Took her where, ma'am?"

She shook her head and grew more husky. "He knew her . . . knew her in the biblical sense. . . . Think of it . . . this dreaming woman, who knows she was formed for a better thing. Vulnerable."

He happened to glance aside at her. Miss Potts had the eyes of Hedy Lamar on the sign in front of the picture show: dreaming and sultry, the signboard read. Miss Potts's hair had come undone. She was Venus rising out of the sea. She didn't see him there at all. It just about scared him into a wreck. He gripped the wheel. He reckoned she thought she was Nancy Hanks with maybe her desires gone into a switch.

The sun was getting low in the west. He guessed he had forty more miles of this. Suddenly she snapped herself out of it. "I have utterly no use for such a man! But we mustn't dwell too much on this. Just let your paper make it clear that Samuel Davis is the father of us all . . . of North and South . . . of Abraham Lincoln and Jefferson Davis . . . of Union and Confederacy. And from that, move on to the Civil War and state its cause."

The lemonade was sour in his throat. "Ma'am, you ain't told me what is the cause."

"Envy, Caleb! The green-eyed monster. One brother reared in poverty, the other enjoying the best of things. Don't you think that Nancy revealed her secret to Abraham? On her deathbed perhaps, if not before. Or her husband did. Or Mary Gilpin, who wrote the diary. Or that friend of hers with the husband Seth. You can be sure he found it of interest, and you can be sure it stuck in his craw. Cain, you recall, was jealous of Abel."

"You mean that Lincoln started shootin' at us just because his brother had more money than him?"

"Not just more money, Caleb, of course. Position. Standing. Gentle rearing on a fine estate, darkies to saddle his blooded horse. A university education."

Caleb guessed he would never have those things, but he knew he would never start a war about it. Miss Potts was humming a little tune. She smelled like his aunt's fruitcakes in the fall, doused good with wine and waiting around till Christmastime.

The closer Caleb got to home, the more he really got depressed. The shovel had slid in under his foot. The pick was shifting with every bump. He thought that maybe just listening to yells had taken the stiffening out of his bones. He didn't see that for all the yelling and all the gas he had any hard down facts to use. He didn't know whether to mention it, but when he drove up to the vine-covered house he gritted his teeth and said it out.

"Well, Caleb," said Miss Potts with a quiet smile. "You show a want of imagination. What we have learned has done a very great deal for me. It gives me the courage of my conviction." Suddenly aware of her tail of hair, with a lashing of elbows she wound it up.

"Yes, ma'am," he said.

She put on her hat and sprang to life. "Let the scholars bludgeon it out," she cried in a voice that echoed her brush with Putney. "You will hand them the weapons." In the fading light her eyes were dark and plump as raisins soaked in brandy. "Let 'em bash out one another's brains. Let 'em hash out every trivial detail. You will give them the bones of history. They can chew on those bones"— she gave him a militant, daring glance —"until hell freezes over!"

He was feeling dizzy — from the force of her words or the scent of her breath. "Ma'am," he said, "I wish you'd take credit for them bones yourself."

"Nonsense," she said. "It's your paper. It's your prize." She bounced it to him: "It's your truck."

He muttered, "My uncle's truck."

"It's your bones."

"Ma'am," he said, "before it gets dark, do you mind puttin' that governor back on. I'm just not sure I know how to do it."

"Of course I will. I was once a forest madonna myself, one with a tool in her hand, you could say. You'd never have caught me cleaning his chamber. I'd have been shoeing his horse instead."

She hopped out then and went under the hood, while he slumped in the seat, his pride of youth, his masculine dignity down the drain.

"Well, Caleb," she said, pulling her hamper loose from the pick, "do I sense a failure of spirit here? See yourself in the line of scrimmage. Tackle this thing. Go to it, go to it, and run with the ball!"

"Yes, ma'am," he said.

"The pen, Caleb, is mightier than the sword. Mightier than the swords of Lincoln and Davis. Pick up your pen!"

"Yes, ma'am," he said.

Tutankhamen Calhoun

I HAVE NO IDEA why Uncle Jeb liked me when nobody else around he could stand. Or why he trusted me to help him out. I guess there was nobody else would do it. My parents had died when I was nine. I had gone to live with him and Aunt Minnie and his sister Aunt Lane and Aunt Lane's daughter named Esther Sue, who Uncle Jeb said would never get married because of her chin, which was hunkered down in her neck a ways. Aunt Minnie was my genuine kin. Uncle Jeb wasn't real kin at all. But he took to me right away when I came. He called me Sister.

"Sister," he said, "You got a honest face. I'm a expert at judgin'. I been bilked enough till let a man put his foot in the door, I can tell you how much he's prepared to steal."

Uncle Jeb owned a lumber mill and made a barrel of money, Esther Sue said. "Which he never, ever, ever spends." Esther Sue had a mouthful of teeth and what she said had to make it through. Uncle Jeb said they were log-jammed. He generally had timber on his mind. But when it come to Esther Sue, I will say up front, there is neither of us got a dab of charity in mind.

Uncle Jeb was already sick when I came. I never knew what the matter was. Esther Sue said he was too mean to live and that's what it was. By the time I was ten he lay in bed a lot, and after a while he never got up.

He liked country music and old-time songs and new ones too. And one day he ordered a big jukebox to keep in his room. Esther Sue said he would never have bought it. A stereo dealer owed for some lumber. Anyway, it was by his bed so he could play it whenever he liked. He sent to the bank for a lot of quarters, which he kept in a hollow post of his bed. He liked to feed quarters into the slot and watch it light up and a record come down. And when his quarters were all used up, he would call me in and give me the key, which was under his pillow, and have me open it and rake up the quarters. And then he would start all over again.

The women complained about the noise. Aunt Lane hated it the worst of all. "I wish just once he would play somethin' sweet. There is so many beautiful pieces composed." She had studied piano when she was a girl, but after her sorrows she couldn't recall how to play a note. Uncle Jeb's music soured her stomach. She held it responsible for all her gas.

Aunt Minnie said, "I'm livin' for the day I can hear a hymn." Esther Sue said that day would never come. She called him a card-carrying atheist.

He hated Aunt Lane and Esther Sue and even Aunt Minnie, far as I could tell. He would say to me, "Sister, I wish you could shut up them squawkin' hens." He wouldn't let any of them in his room. Mattie Lou, the black maid, brought him his meals and changed his sheets and cleaned his bathroom once a week and took him his mail when anything came. Most of his mail he had sent to his post office box in town. I hadn't been there long till he gave me the combination to the lock and told me to get it every single day on my way from school. "I like to be the first to read it," he said.

"Them connivin' hoot owls keeps a kettle goin' to steam the flaps. They ain't good dried when they gits to me." I bet the one did it was Esther Sue.

To tell the truth, I didn't much care for the women myself. They were always in huddles whispering hard like they all had a cold gone down in the throat. Whenever I came in they shut it off. I think it maybe had something to do with Uncle Jeb's letting me into his room.

Uncle Jeb got sicker and yelled a lot. I don't think it was pain. He just hated to die. He said what he hated the most of all was the fact of the women getting his money. "I'm madder 'n hell just to think of it." But I also knew, though I don't know how, that he couldn't bear leaving his money behind. He couldn't bear not being able to take it. One day Aunt Lane said it out at the table. Aunt Minnie agreed, but I had thought all along it was so. I could see his point. Somehow it didn't seem fair to me that if he had earned it, it would ever have to stop being his. I felt them knowing he couldn't take it. I felt them waiting for him to die.

Sometimes when I went to walk in the stores or get his mail and people spoke, seeing who I was, I felt the town waiting for him to die and thinking he wouldn't be taking his money.

It began one day at the end of September. Uncle Jeb's tub had a drain that hardly moved at all. A drip in the faucet outran the drain. But he wouldn't let anyone in to fix it. So once in a while when the tub got full he would send me in to bail it out. Or he yelled for Mattie Lou to do it. Sometimes in the night it overflowed and dripped on Esther Sue in the bed. There was nothing Uncle Jeb loved any more than to hear next day how Esther Sue got wet in the night. "Don't blame it on me," he yelled through the door. "You just ain't learnt to hold yer water!"

I was upstairs sitting around in his room and hearing the drip with a ways to go to the top of the tub. You could tell by the sound how high it was. I was looking at the way the wisteria vine had come in under the window sill and made itself feel right at home. Aunt Minnie said a wisteria vine was the strongest thing in the world there was. If you let it get a toe-hold in your house, eventually it would raise your roof. She knew of a woman had her roof raised off. She didn't suspicion it was there, for Uncle Jeb wouldn't let her in. I wasn't about to stop the thing. I wanted to see what it could do. And I got a definite feeling sometimes that Uncle Jeb wanted the roof raised too.

After his lunch, which Mattie Lou brought in on a tray, he liked to have me pick out a song strictly on my own and punch the button. He liked to guess what it was going to be. Then he liked to have me sit for a while so he could talk about the lumber mill and how he had got the best of his brother, who had wanted to cheat him out of it. Mattie Lou knocked. "What is it?" he yelled. Aunt Lane said he had a powerful voice for a dying man.

"Mr. Calhoun, they's a preacher man out in the yard. He say he come to talk wid you 'bout yo' money."

"My money!" he roared. "You tell him I said to hitch up his britches and make his own."

He went on telling me about the mill. It seemed like he couldn't get enough of that mill and like he was out there yelling at someone sawing up logs and like he was happy doing the yelling and like it had wiped out what all Mattie Lou had come to say.

But after a little bit she was back. "He say he don' want no money a yores. He say he gon' tell you how you can take it along when you dies."

Uncle Jeb got still. "Godamighty," he said. "Them preachers, Sister, is got ways a swindlin' you wouldn't believe." He left Mattie Lou in the hall for a spell. He put on his glasses, which he kept jammed down in the medicine bottles beside his bed. And then he called out, to my great surprise, "Tell him to wipe his feet and come in. You watch him and see that he don't slip nothin' along the way."

Before we knew it he was in the room. He had sneaked in like the wisteria vine. It is hard for me to say just what he was like. Whenever I saw him he seemed to have changed. The least little bit but enough to make me have to look at him hard for what wasn't the same. To tell the truth, he was viney-like. I know he was thin, with an easy way of twisting around. Uncle Jeb put it: he looked for him to wrap himself round the post of the bed and get his hand in where the quarters were kept. His hair I would say was a pewter shade. Though if he happened to be in the sun, I remember it didn't have color at all. Sometimes it was straight, and sometimes the ends of it frazzled a bit, like it had been singed with a lighted match. And I can't for the life of me see his eyes. They moved so fast, always looking somewhere, they were like little minnows flashing out of your sight. He wore a suit that was shiny black as a preacher's suit. I remember that well. He always wore it. And his tie was like a little black string that was always about to come untied. His suit had a strange kind of smell to it. Sometimes it was something I didn't mind, and sometimes the smell of it burned my throat.

Uncle Jeb looked him over as he stood by the door. "Well, you made it inside. What you got to say?"

"Mr. Calhoun, I believe it is," said the man, coming forward and into the room.

"Well, I see you know mine. But you ain't give me yers."

"Rev. Slocum, it is. I am serving the Church of the Golden Word."

"Godamighty," said my uncle, who didn't like preachers any more than religion and was proud of the fact. "That mean you got yer hand in their pocket? I got nothin' to do with churches or preachin'!"

"So I have heard," said Rev. Slocum. "I am new to these parts, but so much I have heard. And it doesn't offend me."

"So what kinda axe have you got to grind?"

"I have a specialized kind of profession. The soul is assigned to someone else. My work is involved with transference of money."

"Transference, I reckon, from me to you."

"Transference of it to another realm where it can be very useful to you. This particular service is provided for those who have earned their money by the sweat of their brow."

Uncle Jeb had himself a good laugh. "I ain't interested in pavin' any streets with gold."

"That of course would be up to you. The point is the money would be yours to dispose of."

"Get outa here!" said Uncle Jeb, still laughing. "I thought I heard it all. But I see I ain't. But before you go, seein' you got energy and no place to put it, you can drop this here quarter into my box. And punch a little button next to 'Honey Lamb Blues.'"

The reverend slid his eyes over Uncle Jeb's hand with the quarter inside and walked to the box. He gave it a stroke and a little punch and the thing lit up the brightest I'd seen with red and blue and orange and green, and a purple color I'd missed before, and "Honey Lamb Blues" came into the room.

Then he turned and without a word he was gone.

Uncle Jeb lay very still in the bed. I could tell that he wasn't hearing the music. He looked even sicker than he had before. When the music cut off he didn't talk. So after a while I slipped away and played with the cat outside in the yard.

"Mattie Lou," I heard him ask when she came for his tray. "You got an idear where that preacher come from?"

"Naw, sir, I don't. I was sweepin' the porch and nex' time I look he was standin' there."

"I ain't hungry," he said. "You take it away. And tell Joe to git me four bottles a likker."

"Mr. Jeb . . . you know likker cain' do you no good."

"You tell 'im, you hear. . . . If you tell Miss Minnie I'll have yer gizzard."

Uncle Jeb drank for I guess two days and cussed a lot. Esther Sue clapped her hands to her ears when she passed his room, in case it was bad. But I listened outside his door when I could. Living in that house and trying to grow up enough to leave, I knew I needed to learn all I could.

It must have been nearly a week gone by. Uncle Jeb was sad or maybe he was mad. It was sometimes hard to tell what he was. He didn't even care about playing the music. He didn't talk about his brother and the lumber mill. I had brought him his mail and was still in his room. I was looking at how the wisteria vine had crawled clear up to the top of the window. Mattie Lou knocked. "Mr. Calhoun . . . I seen that preacher man 'cross the street. . . . Case he don' go 'way, what you want me to say?"

"What's he doin' there?"

"He ain' doin' nothin'. Just standin' like."

He looked at me and then into the ceiling. "You go back and look and if he's still there invite him in."

She gave no sign.

"If you tell Miss Minnie I'll have yer gizzard."

In no time at all Rev. Slocum was with us again.

"You ready to talk business, Mr. Calhoun?"

Uncle Jeb punched his pillow three times. "I got no idear what yer callin' business."

"I told you," said Slocum. "I made it clear."

"Godamighty! Clear!"

"Mr. Calhoun, have you heard of King Tut?"

"Cain't say that I have."

"He was a man with an eye to the future."

"Never heard a him. What you got in mind?"

"Mr. Calhoun, you're about to take a journey of some importance. In a way I would call it a business trip. And so you would like to carry along the tidy sum you have set aside."

Uncle Jeb thrashed his feet in the sheets. "I'm a sick man in no mood to trifle."

"I agree," said the preacher. "You have no time to waste."

I could see that Uncle Jeb's eyes were climbing along the wisteria vine. They were mighty red, I guess from the likker. "It hurts me to say it but I know it a fact. Money is all I ever knowed but it ain't worth nothin' once I'm gone. Not to me it ain't."

"Gone where?" said Slocum. "To heaven or hell? There is little difference if you have the cash."

Uncle Jeb grabbed ahold of his glasses and skidded them on. "You tryin' to tell me it's all the same?"

"In a manner of speaking. But your credit's the thing."

"My credit is always been the best in town."

"Your credit, sir, is worth nothing there. Good deeds are the credit that gets transferred. Surely you've heard all that before. If you got good deeds transferred on the books, you live with the best provided free. Otherwise, sir, you pay for the best. The things you want you must tip someone. It isn't bad if you have the cash. What is known as hell is the state of existing after death with no credit and no money to take its place."

"It sounds like here," said Uncle Jeb.

"Exactly," said Slocum, "but there it's worse."

Uncle Jeb sighed. "I'm listenin'," he said. "But I ain't never hear and I ain't never read and I ain't never dream it up in my head how I can leave here with the least bit a cash."

The reverend was suddenly beside the jukebox. It was actually amazing how fast he could move. "Think about this box and what it can do. You're used to it and you don't see what a miracle it is. That music used to be somewhere else, maybe four thousand miles away, but it got put into that round black plate maybe ten or twenty years ago. You give it the needle and the music is here." He touched the box with a stroke and a punch and the thing lit up and "You Dasn't Leave Me" came out full and strong.

"How did you do that?" Uncle Jeb yelled above the song.

The reverend smiled and all of a sudden was across the room. We listened till the music had played itself out. Uncle Jeb lay looking almost dead. When the record was done, he moved and said, "Sister, there's a bottle inside that box." And he got the key from under his pillow. "You bring it to me."

I did what he said. I always did. If I'd had good sense, but nobody ten years old has got sense, I'd have told him he shouldn't drink any more, especially with that reverend waiting around to get into his head.

Uncle Jeb raised up and took a good long swig and lay back down. "I'm listenin'," he said.

Rev. Slocum moved in and stood at the foot of the bed. "I serve the Church of the Golden Word."

"That mean you run it?"

"It means I serve. Are you familiar with the Bible to any degree?"

Uncle Jeb said weakly, "Get outa here," and barely raised up to get a swig of his likker.

Mattie Lou was knocking at the door with his lunch. "I ain't hungry," he said as loud as he could.

"Miss Minnie say could she have a word with you."

"Hell, no, she cain't! I'm busy now."

He was slap worn out and closed his eyes. I had locked the jukebox and given him the key. But Rev. Slocum slid over to the box again and stroked and punched, and out came the quarters into his hand. At the sound of them Uncle Jeb opened his eyes.

Rev. Slocum was back at the foot of the bed. He tossed the quarters from hand to hand so they made a fine silver chink of a sound. Then he threw them into the air like a juggler, catching one up as another came down. He laid them on top of Uncle Jeb's chest. "You got lots of these in the bank," he said, "and what we have to do is this. We have to get all of it changed to gold. Or as much as you want to take along."

Uncle Jeb stared at him silently.

Suddenly the reverend produced a Bible and held it up. "Mr. Calhoun, here is the Word."

Uncle Jeb sighed and slowly the quarters slid off his chest. "Get outa here, Slocum," he tried to yell, but his voice wouldn't make it. "I been hearin' that hogwash all my life."

"Don't despise the Word," said Rev. Slocum. "It's the only way to get past the Gates with the money you earned by the sweat of your brow." He gave a little jiggle like the start of a dance, while Uncle Jeb had him a draw on his bottle. "Believe me, brother, you'll need it there. Plenty of folks don't have it, you know. Didn't have it here or didn't take it along if they had it here. But it's good to have when you enter the Gates. It makes life easier. Some little service you want performed. Something extra you happen to fancy. If you're there for the rest of eternity you might as well get yourself comfortably fixed."

Aunt Lane and Esther Sue passed in the hall. We heard their voices hush, and then they were listening outside the door. If they hadn't done that, things might have been different. But Uncle Jeb knew they were there and yelled out, "You female buzzards, I ain't dead yet!"

We listened and heard them go away. Then Uncle Jeb said to

Slocum right out, "I got to get this thoroughly straight. What was you tryin' to say about gold?"

"We must get the gold and make the Word. It's only the Golden Word you can use."

Uncle Jeb propped himself on his pillows. "You ain't makin' no kinda sense to me."

"The Golden Word is pleasing to all you will meet up there. We get the money changed into gold, and then we form the gold into pages and then we fill them full of the Word and we have you something that will get you in. And what is more, something you can spend up there. Like a traveler's check. You heard of them?"

"I ain't had time for travelin' around."

"And yet before long you will take a trip."

Uncle Jeb had him another drink. "Wait a minute," he said. "Wait just a minute!" I thought he sounded drunk. "You tryin' to tell me I can get this book past the undertaker, not to mention these womenfolks around? And if I did, you tryin' to say I'm awalkin' outa the grave with it? When I'm some kinda spirit you could spit clean through that couldn't even lift a flea?"

Rev. Slocum smiled. Straight at the jukebox he pointed his finger. "It's like a record. We turn it into something else and turn it back when you get there, man. Except we do it just the reverse. That's the whole trick. One entirely legal, in the heavenly sense. It's beautiful, beautiful, Mr. Calhoun."

"Get outa here, Slocum," Uncle Jeb said. "I ain't that drunk." He put the bottle under the pillow.

Rev. Slocum moved in to the foot of the bed. He slipped his hand up the post with the rest of Uncle Jeb's quarters and made them rattle like seeds in a gourd. "With the record, you see, we take something spirit, the music, you see, and we turn it into something solid. And then we turn it back into spirit. . . . And here we take the gold that's solid and turn it into something that's not, and then at the end we turn it back."

"You got some kinda way this works?"

"Of course," he said. "It's a service of mine."

"And what do you charge for this service, Slocum? You sound like a man has a service charge."

"It's a great satisfaction to me to serve."

Even I could tell what a lie that was. Poor Uncle Jeb, I guessed his brain had given way. Maybe it was drink or maybe whatever was making him sick. Or maybe when he thought of the whole town waiting around for all his money to get left behind, he didn't care. He lay there with his eyes closed tight. It looked like maybe he had gone to sleep. But after a while he said, "Slocum . . . you listen and listen good. I gotta see this damn thing work. I gotta have some kinda demonstration."

"I guarantee you shall have it, sir. And to your entire satisfaction."

"Get outa here, Slocum. You've wore me out," said Uncle Jeb. He shucked off his glasses and jammed them down into all his bottles.

Rev. Slocum turned around at the door. "The demonstration requires gold. A ten-dollar gold piece will do quite well. You have it here by tomorrow early afternoon."

After he was gone Uncle Jeb lay still, but I sensed he didn't want me to leave. So I sat and listened to Aunt Minnie down in the yard below calling the cat away from the sparrows.

Uncle Jeb felt around with his feet. "Sister, find me a cover. I'm feelin' cold."

I raised him a blanket from the foot of the bed. "Sister," he said, "you hand me the phone." It was by his bed, but I guess he was feeling too weak to lift it. I handed it to him, and pretty soon he had the bank on the other end. "You listen, Hiram, and listen good.

I'm sendin' my niece. I want you to give her a ten-dollar gold piece and charge it to me. . . . Well, find one, man. You got connections. You find me one and you give it to her. . . . Well they is done gone on sale, I read it. . . . I don't care what kinda country it is." He hung up all at once. He was out of breath.

Overnight it turned right cold, and Mattie Lou came and made a fire in Uncle Jeb's grate. The reverend was back in the afternoon. I said before that he looked some different each time I saw him. I take it back. It was funny the way he could look the same, and that could top any way that he didn't. His hair was always slicked back on his head and combed up into a bunch at the back, like maybe he kept something hid inside. His tie was always at the very same point of coming untied. His eyes were always like little black minnows you couldn't catch. And he never ever looked at me.

This time he had under his arm a black box about the size of a toolbox. It was kind of long and thin, like himself. Uncle Jeb had him whole cup of coffee and an edge of corn pone. He was sitting up with his glasses on. "Slocum," he said, "this better be good." And from under his pillow he pulled out the piece of money I had brought. It was awfully small, smaller than it seemed to me it ought to be, but pretty and shiny, with writing on it I couldn't read.

Rev. Slocum laid his box on the floor by the door. I think he was smiling. It was hard to tell. "Mr. Calhoun, I must trouble you for an iron now. A plain laundry iron will do quite well."

"Yer fuller surprises," said Uncle Jeb. "I don't gen'ly keep one beside the bed. . . . Sister, run off to the kitchen and get one from under Mattie Lou."

Aunt Lane was on the back porch where I went to get it and I had to tell her it was for Uncle Jeb. She followed me to his room and stuck her head in when I opened the door. "Jeb, if you got ironin' Mattie Lou will do it." I saw the black box on the floor catch her eye. But Rev. Slocum was behind the door.

"Get outa here, Lane. Go back to yer henhouse."

She slammed the door.

He lay back tuckered. "Them buzzards is still a-pickin' my bones."

Rev. Slocum had found a plug for the iron. He opened the black box and pulled out what looked like a piece of brick. Inside of the box it was velvety red. Rev. Slocum put the brick on top of the nightstand. "Allow me," he said and removed to the dresser the glass of water and all kinds of bottles with medicines that kept Uncle Jeb alive. He was careful about it and seemed to have great respect for the bottles. Then he turned around and picked up the tongs for the coal from the hearth. He blew on them hard and dusted them off with the edge of his coat. "Allow me," he said and held out his hand for the ten-dollar gold piece.

Uncle Jeb waited. "Bein' a preacher, you might be partic'lar for some kinda money says God we trust. In case you was, that ain't what we got." Rev. Slocum never said a single word. His hand was still holding itself in the air. So Uncle Jeb dropped the money into it.

The reverend slipped the coin inside the tongs and held it over the coals in the grate. He held it close. If I hadn't known different I'd have thought he was standing there toasting a marshmallow. After a spell he pushed it down inside the coals and the coals flared up. And when they did the light in the jukebox jumped on and off and on and off in time with the flames. I know it happened. I saw the light on the wall and I turned and looked.

Then he took out the money and dropped it on top of the brick on the stand. He covered it up with a piece of something that looked like foil. He spit on the iron and his spit sizzled more than any spit I ever hope to hear. And I couldn't believe it — I could see Uncle Jeb didn't credit it either — but he ironed the gold piece on top of the brick.

"Godamighty, Slocum! What the hell are you doin' to my piece a gold?"

We could smell the metal as he ironed away. The telephone rattled as the nightstand rocked. Sometimes Rev. Slocum looked good and sharp at the foil as if he could see something there we couldn't. At last he raised the foil and there was the coin flattened into a circle that was round as a tiny jukebox record but thinner than paper. Thinner than foil.

"Now I see you can make a mud pie with my money," said Uncle Jeb.

Rev. Slocum whipped out a knife, and with four little slices he trimmed the pie into a square like a pat of butter. "What your eyes behold is a miniature sample page of the Golden Book I shall make for you."

"Godamighty, Slocum, you expect me to believe you can change it into somethin' I can take along?"

Rev. Slocum touched the square with the tip of his finger, and then he leaned over and blew on the metal. His breath was the coldest I ever felt. Then he picked up the coin, or whatever you'd call it now it was square, and slipped to the bathroom. From where I stood I could see him hold it under the drip in the faucet over the tub. "He's holdin' it under the drip," I whispered.

Uncle Jeb yelled, "As long as yer in there fix that leak."

But Rev. Slocum came out with the square little pat shining in his hand and the drip still going as strong as ever. Uncle Jeb sighed. "I never saw a preacher that knowed a damn thing about plumbing," he said.

Rev. Slocum plopped the gold square into the box he had brought along and closed the lid. Mattie Lou was outside the door. "Miss Minnie say tell you she smell somep'n burnin' away in yo' room. She say if you sleepin', wake up an' git out."

"Jesus Christ! You tell them old biddies I can burn down the house if I got a mind. I paid fer it and I ain't dead yet!"

He closed his eyes. "Sister, I need a sip a that rust-lookin' stuff." I found it on the dresser and brought it to him. He drank from the bottle and made a face. "It tastes like nails biled in buckeye juice. This is somethin' I be happy to leave behind. . . . Now, Slocum," he said. "You show me yer trick and it better be good."

Rev. Slocum picked up his box. When he opened it we could see inside the square of gold on the velvety cloth. Then he slammed it shut. He shinnied to the jukebox and stroked it a bit and a record came on, a slow kind of one called "Coal Dust Is Turning Into Star Dust Tonight." It was one that Uncle Jeb liked a lot. When it was over, Rev. Slocum laid the box on the bed and opened it up and the money was gone.

Uncle Jeb said, "Well, I ain't impressed. Far back as I can remember good, folks been makin' my money disappear."

"Your money has changed into something else, something that now you can't see or touch, like the music we heard."

"That's the way it turns out," said Uncle Jeb. "I had me a brother could do it even better than you." He picked up the box and shook it and turned it. He ripped out the red velvet lining inside.

Rev. Slocum was smiling his thin kind of smile. "Send for the record," was all he said. I guessed he was referring to me as the likeliest one they could send to fetch it.

"Well, get it, Sister," said Uncle Jeb. "We gotta see it through." And he gave me the key. I opened the jukebox and then I stopped. The record was still on the plate inside, and on top of the record was the square of gold. . . . I lifted them off and brought them back to Uncle Jeb.

"Sister," he said, "read me out the date. The date on my money said '74."

"I can't, Uncle Jeb. It's got melted out."

"Well, Slocum," said Uncle Jeb at last, "you get out now. I gotta have me a rest before I think."

"Think first and then you can rest in the grave." Rev. Slocum had laid his box on the stand beside the phone. He picked it up and opened it under Uncle Jeb's nose, and there I could see that on top of the cloth Uncle Jeb had torn was another gold coin. It looked exactly like Uncle Jeb's. "Read the date on it, Mr. Calhoun." Uncle Jeb looked and lay back on the pillow.

Rev. Slocum snapped the lid and slipped out the door. I listened for his steps but couldn't hear a thing. All of a sudden the faucet came on like somebody started to take a bath. I was so surprised I couldn't move. Uncle Jeb just said, "Run in there, Sister, and turn it off." And when I came back his voice was low. "Sister, I think we got a stripey black tiger by the tail."

I knew he meant something, but I didn't know what. He lay real still with his eyes closed tight, but he wasn't asleep. I was looking at the wisteria vine. It had crawled clean up to the crack in the wall. I could feel it trying to make up its mind if it wanted to go in or climb some more. "Uncle Jeb," I said, "I bet he coulda slipped it on top of the record some way. He was over there when he made it play." And then I said, "What kinda date did the last one have?"

Uncle Jeb didn't say a single word. I didn't know if he heard me or not. But after a spell he said, "'64." He raised up some and took hold of his medicine, but he put it down. "That was the year my brother like to stole my mill."

"He like to done it, but he didn't," I said.

"He didn't back then," said Uncle Jeb.

"But now he's dead."

"He looked to be dead." I didn't know what he meant at all. In a little while he picked up the phone. "Hiram, I'm sendin' my niece with a written and signed request. I expect you to honor that request in ever last detail. And you know what'll happen to you if you don't. You done lost yer biggest account fer good. . . . And Hiram . . . just in case that don't mean enough, I know what you done with that Gulledge account. You want me to spell it out over the phone?"

School had started. Every day after my classes were over I went to the bank and brought gold coins back to the house in my blue lunch box. Once Joey Hill, the worst boy in school, came by and tried to run off with it, but he dropped it fast when I bit his leg clean through his pants. He just kicked leaves all over the box and said he puked when he saw a girl. That Rev. Slocum was always waiting in Uncle Jeb's room. I gave him the money. He never appeared to look at me. Sometimes I caught his little minnow eyes taking off from my face, but I couldn't be sure that I really had. Mattie Lou had been in and built up the fire with a lot of coal.

We spent the afternoons of the fall with Rev. Slocum heating up the coins and ironing away, making golden sheets about the size of the flat of the iron. He squared them off and held them under the drip in the tub. He kept the pieces and stuck them onto another batch to get melted in, the way Aunt Minnie would save the last little sliver of soap to paste it onto the brand new bar. It was kind of creepy to watch him work. He did it without the least bit of effort, as if it was something he had done before. And Uncle Jeb lay with his skin as white as tissue paper. When he raised up to take little sips of his rust-colored stuff, he gave Rev. Slocum a slanty look. "The smell a yer cookin' is gripin' my gizzard." I saw one day that the smell Rev. Slocum had in his suit was the smell of the gold he cooked in the grate.

Sometimes Aunt Lane or Esther Sue would stand outside the door in the hall, trying to make out if what they smelled was fire in the grate or something else. Then Uncle Jeb would raise his voice. "You got somep'n on yer mind to say? Well, say it and git. Yer givin' me colic." Sometimes when he didn't have breath for that, he would simply yell, "I ain't dead yet!"

In the mornings when I was away in school I think Rev. Slocum wrote on the sheets with a piece of metal that was sharp like a pen. I think what he wrote was out of the Bible. He said it wasn't needful to write it all. Just a little bit would stand for the rest and was all that would be expected up there. Just to show good faith was the size of it. He put the sheets into separate batches, one for each book of the Bible, he said. That's what he said.

I spent most of my time in Uncle Jeb's room, for whenever I left, the women hopped on me like I was a June bug, wanting to know what was going on. "Who is that man?" "What is that smell?" All I would say was I couldn't tell. Esther Sue shoved me into a corner. "You are a bad wicked girl," she said, "and you are going straight to hell."

"I bet you get there first," I said. "You got to have a chin to get into heaven." After that she never spoke to me.

Somehow I didn't know what to think. My mother and daddy were both up there, and I knew they didn't have any book. I think we were poor and the money they had — it wasn't much — somebody had put in the bank for me. Mr. Jarvis, the lawyer, had told me so. But the general idea I got of the thing was that Uncle Jeb was a special case. He had been too bad to get into heaven without something else that was going for him, plus he wanted to get what was left of his money inside the Gate. I liked Uncle Jeb. He was the only one around liked me. They said he was mean, but he wasn't to me. When we listened to records I could almost feel I was back at home with my real-life folks. I hated the thought he was going to die, but if he was I wanted him to have it the way he liked. And so I helped, though I certainly didn't care for running into the reverend each day. The sight of him made the lunch I had eaten that day at school hang around in my stomach for quite some time.

At night we locked the sheets in the jukebox. Uncle Jeb slept with a pistol under his pillow now. I saw it peep out every once in a while. Rev. Slocum said we needed a box for keeping the sheets from getting bent. So Uncle Jeb called up his lumber mill. "Hank," he said, "I need you to make me a little box, eight by eight by eight, with a hinge for the lid. You got that straight? Git on it, now, and deliver it. And Hank, if you spread this around I'll have yer gizzard. I ain't dead yet."

It was Christmas before we got it done. I wish I could say how much money it was got ironed out, but I have no earthly idea of that. From the way Uncle Jeb got all tensed up and felt of his pistol under the pillow, I think it was a good-sized amount. Sometimes he was totally out of breath. Mattie Lou said she didn't see how he could last much longer. I was never real sure how it got worked out so Uncle Jeb would have the box in the grave. I guessed Rev. Slocum would dig him up. Or maybe it wouldn't be buried at all. It was more likely that. I never knew. But Uncle Jeb seemed to be satisfied. So Rev. Slocum didn't come any more and I was glad. But of course it wasn't the last of him.

It was cold outside and started to snow, then changed its mind and settled down to rain. I played Uncle Jeb "My Gussie Was a Hussy" and "The Dogtrot Blues" and "Let's Make Whoopee, You and Me." He never said a word, so I punched him the buttons for "Messin' Around" and "Whango Tango," which could cheer him up if anything could. Then he said to stop and we sat looking out at the dripping trees and I couldn't help it, I wanted to cry.

"Sister," he said, "I ain't knowed you long but I knowed you enough. Ain't nobody but you gonna have my money."

I was so surprised I couldn't speak at first. "Uncle Jeb, you gonna take it along."

"Don't kid yourself. That thin black varmint been livin' in here is a crooked snake. I knowed it time I laid eyes on him. Got a look that puts me in mind a my brother. And he was the slickest I ever knowed. . . . All my life I been toe to toe with the devil. I learnt ever trick he got in his book. You let him come on as fast as he can, and you trip him up with the speed he comes. It's like that judo business, Sister. The harder they come, you give 'em a flip and the harder they fall."

"You gonna do that to Rev. Slocum?"

"You watch me, Sister. This varmint has a notion he is connin' me when all the time I been connin' him. He got the money in a shape right handy for me to use, and I never had to lift a hand. Now," he went on, "the trouble is this. If you git it now, as soon as I'm gone they gonna take it from you. They can hire them lawyers and break any will. I could give you the box, but they'd twist you up so's it wouldn't be worth yer while to live, and you'd give it up." He brooded a while. "No, it gotta be somethin' will fake 'em out. Won't do no good to bury it. Them wolves can smell money a county away. They'll have my whole back yard tore up, and front one too.

"Now, I got a little ol' plan in my head. A post office box is a handy thing. I done rented me boxes all over the state with different names. They goes fer a year. I'm gonna give you the list and the number a the box and the lock combination and when the rent come due on the thing. And I'm gonna leave you a wad a money to pay them rents fer the next ten, fifteen years, little girl, and you gonna have you a good little calendar and keep it straight. Send 'em the money 'fore the rent come due, and send 'em extra in case it went up."

I was trying to understand but I didn't.

"Sister," he said, "I'm gonna make it easy. I got it writ down. Don't worry yer head. . . . Now, what I'm gonna do, I ordered me a box a them envelopes that is thick and tan. I'm gonna mail out the pages a my Golden Book. And there they gonna sit till someday, Sister, you is old enough to take a little trip and rake 'em in."

"Uncle Jeb," I said, "I don't think I got the sense to do it."

"Sure you have. You got the sense. You ain't got the gumption, that's all it is."

I felt like crying. "All I ever wanted was a bicycle."

"You gonna have that and a whole heap more. But you gotta wait so you don't rile up their suspicions none."

Uncle Jeb got weaker after that. The Rev. Slocum hung around outside. Mattie Lou said she saw him there every time she went out to sweep the porch or hang the clothes. Sometimes he would look into Uncle Jeb's window. I saw that twice. He must have shinnied up the wisteria vine. Uncle Jeb slept a lot of the time, but when he woke up he liked to have me there, and then we played songs. It took too much of his breath to talk. Once I was sitting in a chair by his bed, and suddenly the record cut off midway. Uncle Jeb didn't even open his eyes. "Slocum," he said, "you cut that out. I'm a dyin' man but I ain't dead yet."

I looked at the window but I couldn't see Rev. Slocum around. If he was waiting for the Golden Book it wasn't there. Uncle Jeb had mailed it out in little batches, which he had me take to the big post office on my way to school. And I had the money, a great big wad, to pay for the rents, and I had the addresses on a piece of paper. I kept it all hid away in my room behind some bricks of the fireplace. Nobody ever built a fire there.

One day when the trees had begun to sprout, Uncle Jeb up and died in the night. And Rev. Slocum, looking just the same, came in to pay his last respects. One little minute he was with the rest in the dining room, eating cake and stuff that people brought in, and then he wasn't around any more. I guess he was up in Uncle Jeb's room.

After that, I saw him just once across the street. For the first time of all he was looking at me. I tell you that look went down my spine like water from a hose that has stood in the sun, and then it went cold like somebody dropped snow down my back.

Of course, Aunt Minnie and Aunt Lane too were after me to say what Uncle Jeb did with all his money. I lied for a while, said I didn't know. But Aunt Minnie cried till the pins came out of her hair. She said I was her own dead sister's child and she took me in and gave me a home and now we had nothing to keep it going on.

She vowed she was bound to get sick and die. She already had a sick liver, she said, from the hepatitis ten years ago. Mr. Jarvis, the lawyer, with sideburns all the way down to his jaws, came and sat for two hours to get my support. Aunt Minnie got her preacher to pray with me. I cried all the time.

I knew Uncle Jeb would say I didn't have a dab of gumption but I up and told them one spring day. I gave them the list and the wad of money. Mr. Jarvis said I should keep ten bucks. I was glad to have the whole thing over at last. I went upstairs and played Uncle Jeb's records, every one of them. I saw that shiftless, slow-poke vine had made it up to the top at last. I hoped and prayed it would raise the roof. I didn't care if it rained on me. Mr. Jarvis had gone off with Esther Sue to get the money from around the state. But when they got back they reported to us that it wasn't there. Not any of it. Not a single place.

They were looking at me. And I got to crying and couldn't stop. And then one day I didn't care, the way I didn't care if the roof came off. I just didn't care where the money went or what they thought. I didn't care if Rev. Slocum had got it all or if Uncle Jeb had it and was giving the angels big fat tips. I still don't know and I still don't care.

All I really know is that Mr. Jarvis and Esther Sue, who hardly spoke before that trip, ran off and got married in spite of her chin, and everyone in town says his legal business must do mighty well. THEY LIVE IN STYLE!

I know another thing. They got Rev. Slocum on their back for good.

A Good Shape

I T WAS BAD not knowing what you added up to. After he got back from the year in Germany with the army, he used to sit around and wonder what he was. Everybody, even Jakie Reynolds, who was the dumbest guy in the company, had a job or was going to school or knew what he wanted, knew where he fit in.

Already it was 1950, another decade crashing in, and uninvited. He drank a beer for every year of his life since he was out of high school, and it was almost more than he could handle in one evening. In the army you had a job; you had a rating and a number. But god, one thing he knew, he didn't want the army. . . . Sometimes on good days he thought he ought to try for something big. He felt he really had it in him. And then again he thought he might be wasting his time and maybe he should get a job in a hardware store.

His mother was always at him. She wanted him to go in with her brother, who had bought into dry cleaning. "Run a truck for a year," she said, "and then you can be manager. Seven trucks," she said. "Think of that." He tried hard not to think of them.

"What's the matter?" she said. "Don't you want to be a manager?" Sometimes he wished he had stayed in Germany. "What's the matter?" she said. "Don't you want to marry Angela? You can't settle for a job in a filling station and marry a fancy dresser like her."

You would have thought from the way it sounded that she and Angela didn't hit it off. But all the time that he was away she and Angela were thick as thieves. She was always writing: "Today I saw our dear little Angela."

"Well, try it for a year," his mother said then. "Will you try it for a year? What you got to lose?"

He told her, "I got a year to lose." And he went on reading the classified ads.

"Well, what do you want?" She never let go. "Will you tell me that?"

"*Mein Gott,* I don't know!"

"Well, don't swear at me in that fancy language. I'm not in the army."

It was funny the way it came about. One of the classifieds went like this: "Wanted: Men who want a career. Be a Certified Public Accountant. Night classes, accounting. Enroll Now." It didn't appeal to him at all. Just under it was another one. "Chauffeur wanted. Over twenty-one. Good pay. Free time. Call for interview." He'd have a hard time going for that.

But the two together had set him thinking. You could drive some rich character around by day and afterwards take a course at night. That way you could probably pay for the course and find yourself a C.P.A. Not me, he thought. I was good enough with figures in school, but to look at them for the rest of my life! As for driving a bloke with a bad kidney . . . taking orders from someone on top of the heap, he'd had enough of that in the army. It was just that seeing the ads together had made him think that it might be right for someone else.

Then Angela called him on her lunch hour. She did filing for a motor company.

"Hi, kid, you holding out on me?"

"Talk sense, beautiful."

"What's this I hear about you taking a job with the laundry?"

"I'm real pleased you let me in on it."

"No? Your mother said you was going to be manager, but first you was driving the truck for a year to break you in."

"Did she tell you I was driving all seven trucks? They got seven. Did she tell you that?"

"I think she mentioned it. Hey, what's the matter? You talk like maybe I should mind my own business."

"Mom talks too much. She's got too many plans."

"I take it you haven't got any. Look, kid, don't get any idea I'm pushing you. I can make my own plans."

"Will you translate that, please?"

"We don't have to get married."

"Sure we do. Anyway, I've got plans to be a C.P.A."

"What's that? Some Commie organization?"

"Yeah. Better not mention. I'll be over tonight. *Meine Liebchen*."

"You bum. Is that Commie talk?"

He really had been kidding. But the laundry business was making him sick. He could hardly stand to put on a clean shirt. After lunch his mother went to the store and he called the number in the ad for chauffeur. "Call for interview," it said. If the voice didn't sound right he wouldn't show.

The voice was feminine and young. When he told her his business she said, "I'll connect you. One moment, please." A girl at a desk, and she had an accent. It sounded German, but he wasn't sure. He wished she would say something more. Then an old lady's voice spoke pleasantly and firmly, and he found himself promising to meet her by the desk in the lobby of her hotel.

After she hung up it began to seem he had made the appointment for the sake of the girl, for the sake of finding that she was German. For a chance to tell her, *"Guten Abend, Fraulein"* and then to see a spark in her face. He had hated Germany, had known it for a strange, unfriendly land encircled with bars. He had counted the year of it stolen, no less, from his life with Angela. Yet now in the strangest way he was homesick. Not homesick surely for the place itself, but homesick for the looking ahead, when all the future lay sweet and golden and waiting for his hand to take. The ocean had never been there to cross. Just a year, then eleven months, then ten. . . . The time in the boat had been hardest of all, because he had never counted it in.

The hotel was in the better section. He found he had to change buses twice, and before he arrived he'd begun to think that this was another of his mistakes.

One glance and he knew the girl at the desk wasn't German at all. Cuban maybe. Or Puerto Rican, with that dark, dark look. "Miss Pressley is waiting for you by the door." Her accent sounded anything but German. "On the sofa," she added.

"Guten Abend," he replied beneath his breath. And then he realized what it was she had said. "Miss Pressley?" he repeated.

"The lady who needs the chauffeur," she said. Suspicion came into her midnight eyes.

He nodded and started across the lobby. From a distance she looked like any rich old lady. Age had given her body a heaviness. He noticed that her legs and ankles were swollen. She sat with them extended as if they didn't belong to her. As if they were outsized boots she had borrowed and having done with them was waiting for the owner to call. His eyes skipped upward. Her face had escaped the general bulking. There was only a slight puffiness of the cheeks that was not unpleasing and a delicate flush that was like a girl's. Her gray eyes were handsome, with an upward slant.

When he stood before her he saw that tiny lines rayed out from them to her cheeks and temples. He looked away.

She said to him, "Are you the young man who called?"

"James Pressley," he said.

"Pressley," she repeated.

He did not look at her but at the huge fern she was sitting beside. One of the fronds lapped the arm of the sofa and half hid her hand, but a winking diamond caught the light.

"My own name is Pressley," she was saying to him.

He wondered if she expected him to apologize.

"Sit down," she invited.

He hesitated, and then he sat down at some distance from her on the long leather sofa.

She tilted her head and looked at him, in spite of her heaviness, in a birdlike way. "I cannot bring myself to call you Pressley. It would be too much like talking to myself, which I'm inclined to do anyway. . . . And James . . . really . . ."

Her amusement was a small, elegant thing that she placed between them. She might have moved the hand with the winking diamond from under the fern and laid it beside her for him to see. But that he would have understood. He was watching her resentfully.

"No, no," she said, her glance skimming his face, "James is a good name. It's just that . . ." and here she smiled again in the friendliest way. "It's just that James . . . that chauffeurs are always called James. In books, in plays." She invited him to share her amusement.

He looked at her stiffly and then away.

"Don't you see? Pullman porters are always George and chauffeurs are always James. It makes it all seem so much . . . I want to say a parody." She looked at him doubtfully and amended it to ". . . a joke." She entreated him to see it.

He loosened a little. He could almost smile.

"The trouble," she said a little sadly, "is that the whole thing is too much like a joke anyway."

"How do you mean?" he asked, meeting her halfway.

She smiled remotely. "Well, it's just that my affairs are hardly important enough to deserve the energies of an able-bodied young man with better things to do. But there you are. . . ." And she spread out the hand beneath the fern.

"Have you a middle name?" she asked.

He shook his head.

She pondered. "Pick out a name," she said suddenly, as if inviting him to choose a cake from a tray.

He shook his head again. He could not meet her eyes. He looked instead at the fern beside her. Someone came through the door, and the fern leaves moved.

"I dislike doing it, but I shall have to choose for you. I shall have to choose 'William' and William may not be right for you. It may make you uncomfortable. It may make you think of someone you don't like."

He gave no sign.

She went on. "I shall have to choose William because it was the name of my last driver, and it will be so much easier for me. I should end by calling you that half the time anyway."

He looked very briefly into her face.

She became businesslike. "Have you any unpleasant associations with 'William'?"

He was able to laugh. "I guess not." In a moment he added, "I don't know any Williams." He was thinking: Just a hell of a lot of Bills.

And she smiled as if she had read his thought and knew a hell of a lot of Bills herself.

He began to like her. But not, of course, wholly. He guessed he had never liked any one entirely. Not even his mother. Not even Angela. How could you, when you were you and they were they? There were too many things you could never get together on. He guessed what he felt was that you had to be alone.

She was saying, "I have in mind paying you two hundred a month."

He nodded without expression. It was more than he had expected.

She studied him with a faint smile in her slanting eyes. "I suppose I should ask you about yourself. For a reference, possibly."

He began, "I have an army discharge. In Germany I drove a staff car."

"Do you have any questions?" she asked him suddenly.

Across the lobby was the girl at the desk. She was patting her hair in a gesture like Angela's, very much as if it belonged to a kitten. He swallowed. "I had in mind taking a course in a night school. Would you . . . need me at night?"

She sounded sorry. "I'm afraid so. I look forward to concerts in the winter." He felt, abruptly, oddly relieved. Then she too looked at the girl at the desk. "It may help you to know that the job is quite temporary."

He waited, of course, for her to explain, but she went on gazing across at the girl. Abruptly she bent and drew a cane from behind the fern and grasped it heavily. He saw at once that she wanted to rise. He stood and helped her, keeping his eyes from her swollen legs.

She smiled at him, the tiny lines raying out from her eyes. She opened her purse and plunged into it the hand with the ring. "Here are the keys," and she handed them to him. Just like that. "You'll find the car in the hotel garage. Take it for a ride. Do you have a young lady?"

He nodded.

"Take her for a ride this afternoon. Or perhaps tonight."

"Thank you, Miss Pressley."

"And call for me tomorrow. Shall we make it at three? Goodbye, William." Leaning heavily upon her cane, she began to walk slowly toward the elevator.

After that, he was always William. It was funny how quickly he got used to it. There were times when he thought of himself as William. And once when Angela called out, "James," across a room, he didn't answer. She had to call again.

He felt good about putting off the night school. Miss Pressley had said the job was temporary. Afterwards he could decide; he could begin to plan. Meanwhile it was late in the summer, the days were fine, and the work was hardly demanding. Miss Pressley didn't go out every day, but neither did she keep him on the hook. "I won't be needing you tomorrow, William." Then he went to the races just to watch the horses, with maybe a small bet to give it a kick. Or he rang up Angela and they took a late bus to the city pool. Or they went to the zoo and ate the peanuts themselves, sitting on a bench somewhere in the park. It was a little like being in Germany, killing time, waiting for somebody to call for the staff car. In a way he was waiting for Angela still. She had never slept with him. She said she was saving it. Saving it for when? For when he drove his first truck . . . or the seventh truck?

"For marriage," she said.

"It's blackmail, what else?"

"I'm a nice girl, you bum."

He had moved into a rooming house only six blocks from Miss Pressley's hotel. To be near the job, he told his mother. But actually to get away from the talk of it. "I ask you what kind of a job is that when you could manage a laundry!" She reminded him for the seventh time of the seven trucks, and he moved away.

It meant that he didn't see as much of Angela. But when he saw her it was in more style. Miss Pressley had not begun to go out at night. Now and then she offered him the car for the evening. And when he drove it quietly and slowly along a country road in the dark, with Angela's head upon his shoulder and her fluff of clean hair against his throat, he tried not to think of anything at all. He dimmed the headlights until he could not see in the distance, and then the road opened up like a flower. . . . It seemed to him it was the way to live.

At first he didn't think too much about the old lady. He drove her where she wanted to go, careful to avoid the bumps and sharp turns and putting the brakes on all at once. He helped her in and out and handed her things and in general tried to keep her from falling off her piano legs and breaking her neck. She was very game. Once a small truck rammed them from the rear and sent her sprawling on the backseat. He dashed around to set her upright. "Don't bother, William. I'm quite all right." When he handed her her hat she laughed. "A car is not an unmixed blessing. But the horses were far worse, believe me."

That made him realize that she must have been around for quite some time. Now, what would an old lady like that have to live for? She must have lived it up long ago. No marriage, no children, no relatives around that he could see. No health. But money. For gasoline. . . .

At first he wondered where in hell they could drive but to the doctor. He had something to learn.

Miss Pressley, it developed, had a feeling for art. She told him again that she would go to concerts and to lectures when they began in the fall. But now, in the summer, there was the art museum. She said that it helped her through the heat. Did she refer to the comfort of its air conditioning?

On Wednesdays in the afternoon he drove her downtown to the museum. He helped her out at the door and up the steps. Then standing on the step below, he handed her the cane. She gave it a little flourish like a sword and, nodding his dismissal, went through the wide glass doors.

She stayed perhaps an hour, sometimes nearly two, while he waited in the shade, carefully parked so as to see her when she came again through the glass doors. Then he drove to the entrance, mounted the steps, took her cane from her, and helped her cautiously into the car. She leaned on him heavily as if she were tired. But in her face was remote satisfaction, indeed a flush of excitement. She looked younger. Had she been really younger, he would have suspected a rendezvous.

Then on Thursdays, if the day was fine, he drove her with paints and folding equipment to a spot in the country. Always the same spot, a little elevation not far from the road. While she sat in the car he arranged the scene for her, unfolding her chair to face, due north, the line of trees, unfolding one stool to hold her colors, another close by for water and brushes. Then he reached her wide-brimmed hat, a battered Panama long out of style, from the back seat of the car and helped her up the rising ground and to her chair. He did all this with a hardness of the jaw, as if one day his teeth might clench.

While she painted he slouched in the car, his head against the seat, his cap over his face. Miss Pressley had been clear about no uniform. "Wear something subdued." But a cap she liked. Not a chauffeur's cap, but any sort of cap he cared for. "Subdued," she repeated. While he leaned there with his subdued cap over his face—it was a muddy brown and he hated it; it made him feel like an aging golfer—he thought of many things. Of Angela. Of Germany. He had been in such a sweat to get home, and now he wondered. He thought of the accounting class where tonight he might have been sitting at attention with a notebook in his hand.

The fact disturbed him vaguely that he did not want it. He could not wish he were sitting there this year instead of next. He could not even wish it greatly for next year. He thought of Angela again, but his mind began to wander. Sometimes he thought he did not want Angela any more than accounting, and he was troubled in a way that he could not define. Angela had been a point, a fixed . . . star, would you call it? . . . all the time he was away. In all the times he had not known what he wanted, he had been sure of wanting Angela.

And now if there was nothing he could bring himself to want, what happened then?

This happened. He sat up suddenly and put on his cap. He was at the beck and call of an old lady with dough enough to hire him for any stupid thing. He could just see her Panama on the rock above him.

Then, because his thoughts got settled in this muddy rut if he sat for too long in the car, he stepped out and slammed the door behind him and kicked around in the bitterweed and the little white field daisies, which grew below Miss Pressley's rock, and chewed a bit of grass.

Sometimes on these occasions he mounted the rock while she was painting, and she never looked up. He had a feeling she did not know he was around. He wanted to be left alone, and yet it was offensive that she seemed profoundly unaware of him. It was as if he counted for nothing. As if she had hired him — she really paid him decent money — and then found him of no value. Or of not enough. She sat and stared into the line of trees in the distance. She made little sketches with a pencil, erasing much. Then she opened her paint box and poured out water from the thermos into the little jar beside it and dipped a brush into the water and waved it slightly, as she waved the cane he handed her on the steps to the museum. She always fell again to staring at the line of trees, her hand poised with the wet brush in her fingers, as if she were about to write a message on the air.

Try as he might, he could not help staring with her at the line of trees. It was just a bit of wood that moved against the sky and dipped to disappear in the late-summer amber of a rising field, then reappeared farther on to make an arc of deep green, circling toward them down a hill and losing itself again in another rise.

After she had stared it down, she dipped her brush again into the water, then into the paints and into the water and into the paints and onto the paper and into the water. Sometimes he sat on the rock a little way behind her, biting the bit of grass and watching the water in her glass turn green, yellow green, mud green, green mud, till it looked like the bottom of a stagnant pond. And then with a flourish like the flourish of the cane, she tossed it across the rock and into the field below her, where, he presumed, it poisoned the bitterweed and the little white field daisies. She would pour out another glass of water from the thermos, just as if she were pouring herself a drink. Indeed her hand shook and she looked a little crocked.

On occasional Thursdays she inched her chair to another angle and painted due east or west instead of north. Once it seemed to him she painted east-northeast. But always, with an audible sigh, she returned to the line of trees.

One Thursday — he had been with her six weeks — Miss Pressley was obliged to meet a niece in town for lunch (there was a relative, after all), and it was not until the following Tuesday that she painted. Then it was as if she had to make up for the wasted days. The sky was overcast, but she was ready for the car an hour early. She had skipped her nap.

While she painted on the rock she did not seem to notice the steely sky or the nagging wind that whipped the skirt about her legs. He had begun to think of these excursions as her way of passing a fine day in the sun. But today in the sullen weather, she painted with a new intensity. From across the field she was plunged into the trees.

He lay unnoticed on his back in the field behind her rock. The gray sky seemed to press against his eyeballs and the smell of bitterweed was a sickness in his throat. He counted on a date with Angela after he took Miss Pressley home. He tried to think of kissing Angela. But all he could really think of was the view of trees in the distance from the other side of the rock.

He got up at last and circled the rock to the north side and sat beneath it. Here some of the trees were hidden from him, and the fields bulged up in a different way. He studied the scene with a vague resentment. He flattened his back against the rock and raised himself slowly, as if he were a ship coming over the horizon, and the small undulations of the field fell below him and the tips of the hidden trees sailed into view.

Suddenly it began to rain on his face. A fleck here and there like a mild sea spray. Above the distant trees a stain of a cloud had darkened and spread. He stepped out from the rock. "Miss Pressley, it's raining."

She looked up and then down at him. "So it is," she said, almost in wonder. She glanced at the sky and reached for her cane. ·

He bounded up, pleased as a child with the rain. He pointed to where already the line of trees was obscured. He helped her to stand, and the rising wind whipped the skirt about her swollen legs.

She gripped her cane. With her free hand she caught up the small cushion and the portfolio she had held in her lap. She took a step forward and the contents slid out, Half a dozen landscapes blew across the rock. He dashed to retrieve them. One of them sailed into the field where he snatched it along with a handful of bitterweed. As he ran back to her, he quickly assembled them. All seemed to be pictures of the field and the trees. All exactly alike, yet perhaps with a difference he had no time to study. The colors had run and were staining his hands.

He handed them to her. She grasped them carelessly, creasing them against the soft round of the cushion. He looked at her, surprised.

"They don't matter," she said. In her eyes was a glimmer of amused impatience.

Her words and her look were like a whip in his face. For a long moment he could not move. Then he took her arm. The rain struck with force as he helped her into the car. But he did not hurry. Slowly he raised the window beside him. With teeth clenched he climbed back up the rock. If the pictures didn't matter, did the damn paints matter? Did the damn chair matter? Did the damn stools matter? What did all this damn driving matter? Or his job, did it matter? She would damn well stop making a fool of him. He would quit.

But he needed the car to see Angela that night. He did not quit; he nursed his grudge. Driving back to town in his wet clothes, he fondled it, holding it close in his bruised, puzzled breast, while the sober brown cap, soaked through to his scalp, gave off the smell of wet dog on the door mat.

Umbrella in hand, he helped her out at the door of her hotel. She hobbled a little on her swollen ankles. She sighed, "It's the rain. Perhaps I shouldn't have gone out." At the door she paused. "Take the car if you like. And give my regards to the young lady." She smiled and went in without looking back.

He muttered his thanks, but she could not have heard.

It was still raining when he took Angela to supper. "Aren't you a swell!" she said, stroking the leather upholstery. "Does the old lady know it?"

"Know what? That I'm a swell?"

"That you've got her car, goof."

"Hell, I rent it by the hour."

"You liar! How much?"

"Plenty. That's why I can't afford to feed you too good. Don't order much, hear."

"You bum."

They always went on in that kidding way. That long time in Germany he liked to remember the way they had kidded. Affectionate kidding with kisses between. But lately now and then an edge was in it. The kisses were good. The edge was in the words.

In the restaurant he studied her delicate white face with its ring of fluffy hair. Brown hair. Soft and pretty. She spent time on her hair. Too much time, he thought. She was always telling him he couldn't come over because, for god's sake, she had just put her hair up. ("Well, take it down," he would say. "You dope, I can't.")

Her throat, small and white, was the loveliest he'd seen. She always wore something tight around it, something big. Big pearls, big black beads, or a collar of rhinestones. Always earrings to match, and usually a bracelet. Under all that big stuff she looked tiny and fragile. Tonight she was wearing those pink pearls he had given her. She had picked them out. They changed color like bubbles.

He watched her cut her steak languidly and push a morsel between her white teeth. She was a tiny eater. She talked a lot about eating, but nothing tasted really good to her. She left most of it, even candy.

"Eat!" he said to her now. "Eat, kid. Get healthy."

She flashed her teeth at him. "There's nothing wrong with my health, I'll have you know."

"You look puny."

"I like that!" Then she said, after chewing, "You want I should get like that Miss Pressley of yours? Big legs . . . big ankles?"

His face darkened a little; he could not have said why. She had repeated his own words. "She's sick, that's her trouble."

"She's not too sick to go driving, I guess. You want I should look like that?"

"Lay off," he said.

"Hey, what's the matter with you tonight? Did she bawl you out maybe?"

"Shut up," he said.

He made up with her in the car, but it was not too good. He was feeling depressed, and he took her home early.

"Come on in?" she said.

"I better not."

"Well, if it don't appeal to you. . . ."

"I better get air in that rear tire before they close."

"You liar," she said. "You got another date. A swell car like this you can take your pick."

"Oh, sure," he said. And he kissed her slowly to see if it was going to be all right. But while he kissed her he was thinking of lying behind the rock, when he had tried to think of kissing her as he kissed her now. The gray sky was pressing against his eyes and the sickness of bitterweed was in his throat. And suddenly in his mind was the line of the trees. Then the sheets of paper blew across the rock. He chased the little paint-smeared devils through the weeds. And Miss Pressley creased them against the cushion. "They don't matter," she said.

He left Angela at the door and got into the car. So what matters? he said. The damn trees matter. For some damn cockeyed reason she's got to look at those trees.

It had stopped raining, but the wet streets were subtly aglow from the house lights. The black car slid through the night like a panther crushing the puddles kindled with light, crushing the papers running with color into a cushion held to her chest.

Deliberately he chose the road he had driven with Miss Pressley. The stars had come out all over the sky. And the rock, when he passed it, was clearly visible. Through his open window he smelled the bitterweed. Across the field now he could see a portion of treeline. He kept turning his eyes to it as he drove. Once he lost it behind a rise of ground. Then it was hidden by willows looming from the bank of a ditch. He drove on swiftly till the trees were beside him. He pulled off the gravel and thrust his headlights into their midst. A narrow dirt road seemed to wind among them. It looked forsaken and sodden with rain, and he was afraid of stalling the car.

He got out and doggedly followed the road that glinted a silver gray in the car lights. It led in among the trees, looping slyly — he could not be sure it was really a road — till suddenly, perversely it seemed to end. He found himself walking on wet forest floor. Layers of wet leaves. Countless autumns of leaves. He was breathing their mold, an ancient, pungent smell. The lights of the car were filtered through branches. They were outside the world. And the stars overhead were quite shut away.

He stood in the dark grove alone with the trees. They were making sounds. He held his breath, listening. He was hearing the movement of recent rain. Leaf to leaf, each was passing its mist drop, a million leaves swelling the pinfalls of sound, till his face and his hands were wet with their clamor.

Once in Germany, in part of a great forest, he had gone hunting with a friend from his company, and the moisture had dropped on them slowly like this. It had been autumn and the leaves were falling. They were like moments falling. His long year of exile was shedding its days. Here on this midnight at the end of summer it was almost autumn, and the leaves would fall at any hour. He found himself listening for the first leaf fall. The first of all the falling leaves that would take away Miss Pressley's trees . . . and take away the year with Angela, which was to have been the first of many but now in some strange manner had become the year in Germany that he waited to have done with.

He stood among the dripping boughs, hearing the clatter on fallen leaves and the whispered seeping through myriad autumns. He heard the leaf shapes rotting away. He heard his own life losing its shape, moment by moment and year by year.

In the dark of the wood there had lain in wait the savage meaning of these trees.

FOR A WEEK Miss Pressley kept to her rooms. She sent him a message. "William: I am feeling a little ill," she wrote in a strange, uncertain hand that belied the moderation of her words "and think it wise to keep inside for a few days. By all means use the car." Instead of writing, why hadn't she phoned?

His time was his own. He went to the races. But after two days he was restless and waiting for her call. He lay on the bed for a good part of the day and stared at the ceiling.

Angela called him. "Hi," she said. "You sick or something? I kind of worried."

"Busy," he said.

"Old lady got you on the jump?"

"Yeah. Yeah."

"Big social stuff, I guess. You make her give you time off, huh? You tell her what she can do."

"Sure. Sure."

"Hey, you all right? I mean . . . you all right?"

"Oh, sure."

"Well, give me a ring, will ya? I like to know the score."

He supposed he missed the old lady. No, it wasn't that. It was just that after all those months he had a job, and he felt at loose ends when it wasn't there. Maybe, he thought, he ought to check on her. Maybe. . . . Maybe she had never called a doctor.

He ran downstairs to the phone in the hall. He dialed. The desk girl greeted him in accent. "Miss Pressley, please." The phone rang for such a long time that he thought they must have taken her to a hospital. At last she answered.

"Miss Pressley . . . this is William. I thought I'd check on how you are."

"Better, William." Her voice was crisp but weak.

"You . . . you got a doctor, didn't you, Miss Pressley?"

"Certainly, William." In her voice was the glimmer of amused impatience that he had seen in her face before. She seemed to remind him it didn't matter.

"You let me know when you want me," he said.

"Yes, William." She paused. "In the meantime use the car when you like."

"Thank you, Miss Pressley."

He hung up. Where did she think he wanted to go? Apparently the damn car didn't matter either. He'd have liked it better if she had said, "Take good care of the car, William. Don't drive it over sixty." That would have sounded normal to him. As if he had a job.

He returned to his room and lay on his bed to keep from seeing the half-soiled clothes on the chair and the floor and the row of beer cans on the window sill. He had been undressed when, early in the day, the maid had knocked. She had never come back. I live in a dump, he thought savagely. A curtain rod had pulled loose from the wall, and the green net curtain dipped to the floor. It had been so for weeks.

He closed his eyes and the line of trees glided into his mind, curving, dipping in the amber field like blackbirds busy on the fallen grain. If he pressed his eyes with the tips of his fingers, abruptly the line rearranged itself. In a moment the birds took off from the field and the line of them hung in the sky like a ribbon, and then quite swiftly began to recede. "Follow them, William!" Miss Pressley cried. And they raced in her car toward the line of birds. He was glad he had filled up with gas for the chase. He was gaining on them. He turned his headlights into their midst. After all they were trees. He walked among them into the night, and he saw they were full of a strange dark meaning. In the stillness he grew aware of their sound. The last of the rain was stirring in the leaves. In an agony of listening he strained to hear. What had seemed the rain was a first faint chuckle high up in the boughs. Then it slid downward through branch after branch till he stood there soaked in Miss Pressley's laughter.

Something was knocking against the door. Someone was calling, "Telephone, Pressley." It had a strangely disrespectful sound, until he realized that he was Pressley. He got up and opened the door and went down.

"All right," he said into the telephone.

"William," said Miss Pressley, "I've been thinking since you called. I think I'd like to go out tomorrow if the day is nice."

"You . . . think it'll be all right, Miss Pressley?"

There was a pause as if she had not understood. "Well, there isn't much time left," she said at last. Did she mean till fall?

"That's right," he said.

"Yes . . . the usual time, William."

"All right, Miss Pressley."

There was another pause. "You hadn't planned something with your young lady, had you?"

"No, I hadn't, Miss Pressley."

After she hung up he remembered that she had not said where she wanted to go, yet the place had been between them like a secret they shared.

Going back to his room, he felt strangely light. Like getting on the boat for home after the year in Germany when the fear had grown in him that Angela would die, or marry someone else, before he saw her again. He had been afraid that Miss Pressley would die.

Back in his room, he tore the sagging curtain from the wall and tossed it into the corner. He was almost happy.

That night he grew afraid that it would rain. But the following day was very bright, with a special sharp blue in the grain of the sky and even a little dry tang of autumn. Miss Pressley painted with a pink scarf wound about her throat, the ends of it hidden by the brim of her hat. Except for her paleness she seemed the same. But even the paleness disappeared in the sun.

He lay behind her on the rock, closer than he had ever ventured before, with the sun on his face and his eyes closed. Through his eyelids the sky seemed to pass and to fill him, as if he were washed and drowned in its blue. He could hear the faint swirl of her brush in the water and the sound as she shook it free. He was sure that he heard the plash of the drops as they struck the rock quite close to him. Again he was among the trees in the dark and their mist fell on his face and hands.

He got up suddenly and stood beside her and looked with her into the line of trees. And he said, without having rehearsed it at all, "What's so special about those trees?" He was tense with the effort to be casual.

She looked up at him through her gray, slanted eyes with the raying lines now deep in the sunlight. She smiled faintly as if she had waited for him to ask. "Well, they have a shape."

His eyes went past her to the edge of the rock. "How do you mean?"

She dipped her little brush like a swallow and swirled it in water. "Well, it's rare to find a perfect shape in nature. One thing, perhaps. One tree. But not a group of them." She looked up at him, amused and kind. "Not all together." Then, seeing his face, she said, "I'm afraid it's a little hard to explain!"

He dropped his eyes. It was quite impossible to ask her more, but his throat was dry with wanting her to go on. He was almost angry.

"Look," she said. "Take a day. Any day. Some of the moments in it are good. But put them together. The day they make is hardly perfect." She drew her brush from the water and traced a pale curving line the length of her open palm. "Or take a life," she continued. "Some of the days, maybe even a year of it, will be good. But put them together . . . will they have any meaning? Will they make a shape?"

She studied him briefly. "It's the shape we are after." And she said it, said "we," as if she drew him into her search, as if indeed he made part of her shape.

He laughed uncertainly for want of an answer.

She said to him gently, "If there is no shape we must make one, William. It takes practice, practice. You have to find what a shape is before you can make one. You must look for shapes."

Her voice turned gay, and she flung the green water out of her brush. "If you find a good shape," and she jabbed her brush through the field at the trees, "hold on to it, William. Don't let it go."

She swirled her brush in a gluey gobbet and made a green oasis in the desert portion of the pad on her lap. He felt dismissed. But she looked up suddenly and said to him, "Now, take those trees. Each one makes a pleasant enough shape, I think. Nothing special, you know. But put them together. . . . If you should go there and walk among them . . . what would be there? What would you see?" He held his breath. "You must look at them from the right place."

Then she said, "Where I sit makes the shape. Where I look."

He stood without moving, hearing the swish of her brush in the water. He hardly knew what he had waited to hear, but he was stunned with disappointment. He stared across the field at the line of the trees. He asked himself if she could have known that one night he had wandered homeless among them. He asked himself if she were not a little balmy. But he asked it to give himself time to think. And the shape of the trees burned into his mind.

She painted on without looking up. At last he left her and sat in the car. He lowered his head against the seat and tried not to think. From the time he had been a little boy, thinking about things had brought him trouble. It was better to kiss Angela than to think about her. In Germany he had thought too much. Miss Pressley made him think too much. He closed his eyes and tried to start over with Angela. At first she had been like a hand at his throat. Slumped in the car now, he drifted with her.

Suddenly he was aware that it was late, and he looked at his watch. He got out of the car and climbed the rock. Miss Pressley sat with her head thrown back. Her hat was caught on the arm of the chair. Her picture had fallen away to the rock.

He saw her there with a clutch of fear. "Miss Pressley?" he said. As if in answer a puff of wind blew her skirt against her swollen legs, and one end of the scarf fluttered loose like a butterfly. But she did not stir. Now there was nothing to keep him from drifting. He would drift with Angela till the day he died, and the drifting and dying would run together like Miss Pressley's painted trees in the rain. "Miss Pressley," he heard himself calling to her.

She opened her eyes.

"What is it?" she said at last from a distance.

He fell on his knees beside her chair and he could not speak.

She looked at him with the old shadow of faint amusement as if she would tell him this too did not matter. "William," she murmured to him at last. She closed her eyes, but in a moment she opened them and smiled past him into the late summer day. "Something has troubled me just a little." She waited a while. "I took your name from you. . . . It wasn't quite right." Her eyes rested on him.

He tried to swallow. "No. No. . . . I liked it. Liked William."

She shook her head. "But it made you different?" She was asking.

"Maybe. Maybe so. It's all right."

"You're quite sure?"

He nodded.

She looked around her at the sky and the rock. He noticed she did not look at the trees. "Then I think I'll go home."

On the drive back she seemed to be sleeping. When he helped her out at the door of the hotel, she said to him, "William, come up with me. I have something for you to deliver for me."

Her rooms were on the floor above. He would have waited outside in the hall, but she said, "Come in, William. I'll be only a moment."

He stepped inside for the first time. It was new to him, this fair-sized room with books lining three walls and the fourth wall hung top to bottom with pictures. On a table by the door was a small marble figure of a young man diving. While she left him alone he looked at the figure aslant in space. The bare feet gripped the edge of the rock. Down the naked body coursed marble drops so real, so wet that he put out his own hand to touch them gently. And again he walked among trees in the darkness and knew the rain on his hands and face.

Then she came out of another room and handed him an envelope. It was sealed. "It's for your young lady. I'm afraid I haven't the time to wrap it." A tremor was in the hand that held it.

He took it in silence. He could feel a rounded object inside. She had asked him before to return a purchase, and now he'd supposed he was here for that.

"She might like to know that it came from Venice. It's something I used to wear," she said.

"You . . . you're sure you want to give it away?" He could think of nothing else to say.

"Perfectly sure. Goodbye, William. It was a pleasant afternoon."

"Goodbye," he said. But he stood without moving. He was looking deeply into her face, as not since a child he had looked at a face, as never once had he looked at Angela's.

"What is it, William?"

"Will you . . . do you think you'll be all right?"

"Of course I will." She began to smile the familiar way, but he turned from her quickly and went outside. In the hall with the envelope in his hand he remembered he had not thanked her for it.

The girl at the hotel telephoned the next day. He was hearing the alien sound of her voice and trying to make the words she said belong to another time and place.

After the call he sat by the window. The maid had been in and retrieved the curtain and laid it folded across the dresser. The envelope lay beside it now. He tried to recall Miss Pressley's face, the way it had been in that one deep look. The autumn would never come for her, the leaves would never fall for her, the trees would hold their shape for her, as she had shaped his hours and days. She had not waited or told him enough. Already he felt himself adrift and losing his name, his chosen name.

After a time he got up and took the envelope. He tore it carefully at one end and slid the contents into his hand. He stared at it with a kind of hunger. It was like a raindrop mounted in gold. He knew nothing of gems, but the stone itself of the deepest azure was caught to a chain by three leaves of gold that seemed to have formed the blue drop as it swelled. He could not imagine Angela wearing a thing so fine. Nor taking off for a thing so real the hollow bubbles he could crush in his hand. Like the bright, fragile balls of a tree for Christmas they were hung from her throat, her wrists, her ears, as if she had known she was for a season.

He swung it against the light from the window. Now the golden leaves seemed a part of the stone, embedded for centuries deep in its heart. The sharp autumn blue of it reached to fill him, as once the sky had washed over and drowned him. Again he lay on the rock in the sun. He lay across from the line of trees.

He folded his fingers over the stone. If you find a good shape, hold onto it, William. To find what it meant would be like walking on fallen leaves in the dark of night. Till the search itself had become a shape.

One Day in the Life
of a Born Again Loser

It was not as if Theron Estes had been in jail for a long time. It was ninety days. And it was not as if he had been there before. It was the first time, for godsake. But when he got out in November, his wife had picked up and gone, taken off and left him with the children. He never even saw her. All he saw was a note that read: "I had enuff its your turn."

Felicia, who was nine going on ten and in the fourth grade could spell better. Josephine was five and in preschool. At least they were not around till three o'clock in the afternoon. He needed time to get the jailhouse out of his eyes and his mind. And he needed time to think what he was going to do. The tubes of the TV had withered and died, but he hardly missed it. Things were that bad. The rent and utilities were paid through December, but after that the whole family, as far as he could tell, was going down the drain. Excluding of course his wife, who was probably lapping up the luxury in her mother's trailer, wherever it was parked, sleeping in her curlers till ten o'clock in the morning, eating sausage links for breakfast. Sometimes he had the feeling that if he looked in the mirror, instead of seeing his face he might see himself walking out the door and never coming back.

Josephine did crayon pictures of dragonflies and rabbits, which she promised she would sell when the rent gave out. His wife had left a small, undetermined amount of money with Felicia and told her to keep it hidden, which she did, and make it last and last and spend nothing for beer. Every two days Felicia went to her hidey place, took out a little cash, and walked to the corner grocery. On the way home she bought a newspaper. Then she put on her glasses and she and Josephine, who couldn't read, consulted the classified ads hunting for a job, any job, for Theron.

It was humiliating to have his two kids discussing his capabilities. He turned them off when he could. But when they both agreed on an ad and approached him with long faces, he usually gave it a try. If he didn't, Felicia dished up a plate of canned limas and said that was it. She had learned from her mother to use food as a weapon. He used to drive a laundry truck, pick up and delivery, but the job had gone smash about six months ago.

Well, of course they wanted references. They all wanted references, and that was the end of that. When this was explained to Felicia, she looked at Josephine over the top of her silver-rimmed glasses, which one of them had sat on and bent out of shape. And before long the two of them came up with a reference written on ruled paper with heavy black crayon: "This man is capable of anything."

Time passed, as time will, and before he knew it Christmas was a problem. No money for presents; that went without saying. But no money either for a Christmas dinner. Felicia spent time alone in her hidey place and announced it would have to be lima beans and Kool-Aid. Josephine looked at him with large, glooming eyes full of tears. She could fill up and spill over any time, like her mother. She was saving her six gumdrops from the preschool Christmas party for their own Christmas meal.

He tried to get a job as department store Santa, but they wanted a reference, for godsake. And a health certificate, which would cost him twelve dollars, which he didn't have. They couldn't let the kids climb onto your knee unless it was certified free of germs.

Four days before Christmas the ad appeared. Felicia and Josephine were waiting when he returned from a walk. School was out for the holidays, so of course they were home and climbing all over him.

Felicia read it out: "Lady of refinement desires to cook Christmas dinner for gentleman of discrimination. References exchanged. Call 839-6603."

"Where'd you get that?" said Theron. It sounded like something from ninety years ago, but there it was in yesterday's paper.

"What's discrimination?" said Josephine.

"I'm not sure," said Felicia.

"Has Daddy got it?"

"Daddy's got everything except a job."

For a little girl Felicia could be tough as nails. She could top her mother at cutting him down to size. Sometimes he was sorry for the man she would marry.

It was obvious from their faces that they were into this deep and were not to be put off. But he couldn't see the sense of it until they explained. He would get himself chosen by this lady of refinement. She would cook for him a fantastic meal. She must like to cook or she wouldn't spend money on an ad like this. And if she was really a nice lady, he would tell her about his children, and she would be so happy to fix them up a plate from all that was left over. But if she wasn't nice he could say, "Oh lady, this is so good! Could

I have a little more?" And when she got back from the kitchen with it, his pockets would be full.

When you got down to it, this wasn't going to be a hell of a lot different from what had landed him in jail. And when he tried to explain this, not without satisfaction, Felicia looked grim and determined. "They'd never get a conviction."

Now, where did she learn an expression like that? Sometimes she really scared him. Besides, she reminded him, she and Josephine were too young to be arrested. "But I'm not," he said.

"But you ain't going to eat what you put in your pockets." She was sure to be a lawyer, what else? he thought.

Josephine looked worried and her eyes began to brim. "Don't get yourself in no more trouble, Daddy, please."

But Felicia put her down. "Nobody ever gets in trouble for gettin' his children somethin' nice to eat on Christmas."

He reminded them about the reference to references in the ad. But Felicia reminded him, "We made you one Daddy. I hope you didn't lose it."

Josephine whimpered, "I missed you, Daddy, all the time you was in jail."

So to get them off his back he did make the call. The phone rang so long that he almost hung up. But then it stopped and a woman's voice said, "Yes?"

Felicia and Josephine were breathing in his face.

"I'm callin' about your ad in yesterday's paper."

There was a long, long pause. "Are you callin' to get your name on the list?" She sounded far away, like maybe long distance.

"List?" he said. "What list?"

"The list of gentlemen who would like to eat my cookin'."

Felicia and Josephine were nodding furiously. "I guess I am," he said. "What do I have to do?"

"You have to answer three questions. First, are you employed?"

He didn't like the way it was going. But Felicia and Josephine were in agony before him. "I'm between jobs," he said. "It makes me hungrier," he offered.

"Second, are you married?"

"I'm between wives," he said. The girls were stricken. "It makes me hungrier," he said.

"Third, what is your favorite food?"

"Cake," they whispered. They were climbing all over him.

"Cake," he said.

She took his name and his number. "I'll be in touch," she said. The girls were ecstatic.

"Listen," he said. "It's some kind of promotion. It's probably a restaurant drumming up some Christmas trade."

Josephine thought it sounded like a rich lady with extra food.

"It's promotion," he said. "You can bet on it." Then he explained, "There are people in this world who'll try any kinda lowdown trick to get your money."

"You don't have any," said Felicia.

"She don't know that."

"She knows you don't have a job. That means you don't have any money." Felicia could put one little fact in her slingshot and hit you between the eyes. She added wistfully, "She sounded like a nice kind lady to me."

"Like your mother?" he asked.

They both began to cry, and he was sorry he had said it.

"It's a promotion," he repeated. Then he went for a walk because he couldn't take any more at the moment.

When he returned the girls were beside themselves. The lady had called back and left word to get in touch. "You see?" he said. "She's afraid I'll get away."

Nothing would do but he must call the number.

"I'm happy to inform you that you have been selected from a list of forty."

"Why me?" he said.

"You qualify," she said.

"Why me?" he said "Why should I be so lucky? Level with me. What's behind this?"

"Congratulations!" she said. And she gave him an address.

"Is this a restaurant?" he asked.

"No, it's not. Be here at twelve on Christmas Day."

Josephine was turning somersaults into the wall. "I love you, Daddy. I missed you, Daddy, all the time you was in jail."

Felicia got her needle to mend a hole in his sweater and brought him the last of the tangerines.

"It's a restaurant," he said. "They'll hand me a menu that says twelve-fifty. Then what do I say?"

Felicia was biting off thread with her teeth. "You can say, 'This wasn't what I had in mind,' and come home."

He couldn't argue with that.

Felicia had a map of the city that she kept with her marbles and her pulled-out teeth, and she knew how to use it. She worked him out a route by foot and by bus, and on Christmas Day she gave him the money for his round-trip fare. "Now, don't get lost," she said. She had washed and ironed him a shirt, in a manner of speaking, and brushed off his jacket.

"Don't get in no more trouble, Daddy," Josephine implored. "I missed you, Daddy, all the time. . . ."

"Shut up," said her sister. "You're makin' Daddy nervous."

"I don't want Daddy to get hisself locked up."

Felicia ignored her. She advised him to brush his teeth real good and then to smile a lot. There was something about women of any age, just to watch them operate, that chilled his blood.

Well, it got to be Christmas. Felicia put seven raisins a piece in their breakfast cereal. He was glad to get away. He left Felicia braiding a red ribbon into Josephine's hair. He was mad at his wife, really hard down mad.

The place wasn't all that easy to find, even with the map Felicia had drawn. He changed buses twice, then walked for a quarter of a mile into a district that seemed to him risky. There were lots of alleys with cats in the garbage. Kids on new skateboards almost upended him. A firecracker exploded under his foot. A woman threw sour milk on his freshly polished shoe and his sock got wet. His nerves were half shot by the time he found the number and climbed the three flights of littered stairs. She wasn't going to be a rich lady, that was for sure. He was tired and hungry. But mostly he was mad at his wife for leaving. He hoped she was starving in some fourth-floor dump. His theory about the restaurant was beginning to be replaced by a crazy hunch that she was behind this, maybe even behind the door on which he heard himself knocking. Her idea of revenge. Or maybe her idea of a good way to end her little adventure. How she had managed the details didn't interest him.

When his knock produced nothing, he knocked even louder. Maybe she had gotten him all across town to a vacant room, just to get even because he went to jail. But suddenly the door opened and he was staring into the face of a woman, a hard down stranger. She was taller than he, and he had to look up. Over forty, he thought. Way over. Hefty, all muscle. Her black hair was bushed up and covered with a net. Her face was large and looked pink, overheated. She was smiling broadly with her lips pinched tight. Godamighty.

"Well, well, well, well," she said, coming on strong. She looked him over, her hand on the door. Her eyes went all the way down

to his sour wet sock and back up again to the top of his head. She
had a hole in her chin. She sneezed with violence, and he drew
back a little, trying to keep dry.

"Well, come in," she said. She wiped her eyes with her sleeve.
"You're lettin' in the cold."

He slid past her into the room, catching his foot on a beat-up
suitcase parked by the door. "You're late," she said, smiling, her lips
pinched again, and looking him over for the second time. She
slammed the door shut with the back of her foot and advanced on
him slowly while he gave way before her. "I'll bet you never had
a Christmas like this. I ask you seriously, did you ever have a
Christmas like this?"

"I haven't had it," he said.

She shook with silent laughter. "Well, now, this is going to be
the most adventuresome Christmas you have ever had." She was
wearing a white dress with buttons down the front. A uniform, he
thought. The dark red stain on the bosom he hoped was cranberry
sauce and not blood. "Well, now," she said, "I bet you're hongry
as a jackrabbit. Sit down or walk around or lie down, whatever
suits, and I'll get it on the table, and then we can visit. I never try
to visit with a hongry man. But first . . . first I'll bring you a little
somethin' to put you in the sperrit." And she left him.

He stood still in the middle of the room, conscious of the smell
of food, not wanting to look around but doing it anyway. The
furniture seemed to him considerably run-down. There was a TV
in the corner with a hole in its face. The climate was uncomfort-
ably warm, but of course he was heated up with climbing the
stairs. She returned to him presently with a water glass of something dark brown in color, which she said was elderberry wine.

"Take a sip," she ordered.

He did, and with an effort controlled his face.

"Ain't it good? It'll put you in the sperrit. Loosen you up."

"It's nice," he said. He thought it tasted like rubbing alcohol and peanuts.

She left him with the bottle, and then he could hear her banging in the next room. In the room where he stood a card table with a battered top was set for two. He walked around and poured half his wine into a vase on the mantel. Above it in a frame was a membership certificate for the National Geographic with the name of Hallie Battersea inscribed in black.

She surprised him from behind. "Here's somethin' to keep you occupied. Really pin your earflaps back to your skull." She handed him a *Home Medical Encyclopedia*. "In livin' color," she said, and she disappeared again.

He opened it to a picture of a pancreas in hemorrhage and shut it quickly.

Then she was back with her left arm covered with plates like a short order waitress. The whole meal, it seemed, she had loaded on one arm. In her right hand she carried another bottle of the wine. Then she arranged the plates and poured herself a drink.

"Sit down," she said "and we'll have ourselves a toast. Let me fill you up. Wanta get you in the sperrit." She filled his glass again. He couldn't help seeing that the food was slim.

They sat down, but suddenly she popped up again. "'Most forgot the music. It helps the digestion." She slithered a record player from a pile of newspapers in a corner of the room and fiddled with it briefly. Then a male voice came out at him loud and strong, in . the nose:

"I fou-u-und you in the haystack all alo-o-one."

She sat down again. "Ain't it beautiful!" she said. "You got an ear for music?"

He let it pass. She raised her glass and smiled broadly, revealing a missing tooth to the right of center. But she quickly put her hand up to cover the gap. "Now, what'll we drink to?"

"Anything you say."

She thought for a moment. "Let's drink to the whole damn holiday season." She laughed fit to kill, a knuckle of her finger where her tooth had been. "That includes Happy New Year." She took a swift drink, spilling a little on the front of her dress just over the red stain and turning it the color of an overdone taco. "That includes the hay!" She was hooting at him above the singer, who by now had for back-up a dozen male voices and full orchestration. "You got anything else you wanta include?"

"You covered it," he bellowed.

She passed him something which she said was a condiment. It might have been anything. He took a little. The voices had shifted to a lively ballad:

"You'll be so-o-ory you stole my Honda
When the buzz-buzz-buzzard buzzes round your head."

Lost in the music she began to eat. He started in himself. After one mouthful he knew what he had. In a corner of his mind he had known it all along. He had a turkey TV dinner spooned out of its foil and onto a plate. His wife had made him the living world authority on TV dinners. He could spot the aroma of one at ninety paces and tell you its brand and its Christian name.

He began to listen to the record, what else? Some loser's best friend had made off on the loser's Honda with his wallet, his watch, and his woman, in that order, and left him with the kid.

She hummed a few bars. Some of her black hair escaped from the net and bounced on her brow to the beat of the music. She looked at him from under it. "You seem like a quiet man. I like a quiet man. You can't fool a quiet man. Thinks deep," she yelled.

A woman shrieked into the room from the record: "Take off your Adidas when you trample over me," and repeated it, pleading, an octave below.

"You Miss or Mrs. Battersea?" he finally asked.

"Oho!" she cried, and she glanced at the framed certificate over the mantel. "I'll bet you're a private eye, what d'ya know." And she laughed for a while. "No, that was a friend of mine died last spring. I wanted a little somethin' to remember her by. One kidney went, and six months later the other went boom."

"That's too bad," he offered.

"I bet we got it right over there in livin' color." Her eyes fished for the medical book he had left on the mantel. "Dandy little book. Helps to pass the time."

He silently observed that she had neglected to pull back the foil from the mashed potatoes for the last twenty minutes to let out the steam. The woman in the record was really letting out the steam, building up to a seizure on account of the Adidas. Listening to her, he could hardly swallow:

"I-I-I can cover up a bro-o-o-ken heart
But not your treadmark on my chin."

The record stopped with a screech. Then suddenly it was back in the haystack again.

"I didn't get your name," he finally said.

She stopped with a forkful of peas on the way to her teeth. "Well, now, it don't make a damn bit a difference as long as I did the cookin'. Drink up," she ordered and filled his glass.

He was thinking how he might talk her out of a couple of frozen dinners for Felicia and Josephine. He hoped he wouldn't have to get her in the hay to do it. He was beginning to feel a little crazy in the head. "What'd you say this was?" he asked, holding up his glass.

"Plum brandy," she said and filled him up again. He was practically sure she had called it something else before. He had trouble bringing it into focus. He heard himself saying, "You called it somethin' else before."

She fixed him with her eye and smiled her tight-lipped way. "Well, now, in a gormay situation I always serve two kinds."

He had to stifle a yawn. "Tastes the same," he said. It bothered him that he was getting sleepy and at the same time more uneasy. He tried to focus on the fellow in the haystack but the guy was getting on his nerves.

> "You t-o-o-ld me you were looking for a needle in a haystack
> And I couldn't let you l-o-o-ok alone."

To the beat of the music she slapped the hole in her chin. And thrusting out her lower lip, she puffed her hair from her forehead in two-four time. She winked at him broadly. "Don't it put you in the sperrit?"

He didn't feel up to what he thought was coming.

But then he heard her asking him, "Do you like children?" She called them "chirren."

He thought about it, chewing. "I never thought about it," he said. "Think about it," she said.

He didn't know what to say. Finally she simpered, cocking her head toward him, her hand covering all her teeth. "I'm sure you love chirren. I can tell you do." She didn't ask if he had any, so he asked if she did.

She smiled a little, still hiding her teeth. "That's for me to know and you to find out."

He looked at his food, what was left of it. Suddenly beneath his feet came a burst of vibration like a trip hammer gone wild. He dropped his peas in the brandy.

She looked up and smiled sweetly. "I got an old bat lives under me has no ear for music. You hear that racket? What she does, she straps a vibrator to the handle of her broom and slaps it to the ceilin'. Just ignore it," she ordered. "Hang on to your garters."

The record was stuttering. She stood up and stamped her foot hard on the floor. He held on to his plate. The needle leaped several grooves; the record died, then wailed itself back into the haystack again.

"Maybe you better turn it down," he suggested.

"Not on your tintype!" she roared with glee.

She sat down and watched him while he trapped the last bite of dressing as it danced on his plate. She tapped her foot to the music and sang a phrase or two with the owner of the Honda, who by then was coming on with a stammer and a sputter. Abruptly she got up and turned down the buzz-buzz-buzzard to a whine and a whimper and sat down again. The rattle beneath him went on for a while and then stopped. The soles of his feet were tingling. She hiccuped twice.

Then she said, "I have a teeny tiny favor." She was beaming at him, and he tried to focus on her. Here it comes, he thought. He must have said it out loud from the look on her face.

She said as sweet as could be, "I can tell you're obligin'. I always count on a quiet man to be obligin' more than most. . . . Well, I have these chirren. It's why I ask if you like chirren. And this bein' Christmas, I thought you wouldn't mind puttin' on this silly ol' suit for a coupla minutes and makin' their day. Oh my, they would love it." She hiccuped again.

"What kinda suit you have in mind?"

"Well, now, it bein' Christmas, it would be a Santa suit."

He closed his eyes to rehearse what it was she wanted him to do. He shook his head slowly. "Wait a minute . . . wait a minute. Gotta have a health certificate." He had some trouble with the final word.

"You look as healthy as a jackrabbit. But have another drop of sperrits, just in case."

"Anyway," he said, "they'd spot me as a fake."

"I don't believe it!" she cried. "A quiet man like you! I can tell you got a real way with chirren. It's a gift."

She stood up suddenly, almost dumping the card table into his lap. "If you finished. . . ."

"Some coffee," he muttered. "Get my head straight."

"Oh, absolutely," she said. "I'll be gettin' it ready while you're puttin' on the suit." She took him by the shoulder, and before he knew it he was in another room, and the door was closed. He focused on a bed and a Santa suit on top. All he wanted to do was lie down on the bed. Instead, he sat down on it with his head in his hands.

"How you comin'?" she called.

He didn't answer, but he rummaged around and found the pants of the suit and tried to pull them on. He could hear her at the door. "They're too tight," he yelled.

"Well, now," she said, coaxing. "A private eye like you could figure out what to do. First, you take off that good-lookin' pair of pants you got on."

He thought about it for a while. At first he was inclined to tell her to go to hell. But then he remembered that he had to talk her out of the frozen dinners for the girls. So he took off his pants, what else? It was chilly in the room. He found that by tugging and popping a few threads he could get the Santa pants on, but there would be no sitting down or anything like that, or hardly any walking. Then he took off his jacket and replaced it with Santa's.

She barked through the door. "The beard is in the pocket." He found it and stuck it on.

The door opened a crack and then another crack. "Beautiful!"

she brayed. "It chokes me up to see you. I mean it," she said. "But where's the hat? It's in the other pocket."

He found it and put it on. He wasn't too drunk to feel like a first-class number-one fool. He felt like a prostitute. Jail was better. They allowed you some honor while you rotted in your cell.

"Come on," she coaxed. "It won't take but a minute." She straightened his hat and buttoned up his front. "My, it takes me back. Brings tears to my eyes." He found his hand in hers, and he was being guided through a doorway and into a room that was hung with sheets and other laundry. It smelled a little sour. Then she pushed him through the sheets, which were damp on his face and made him think of the time he had backed the laundry truck into the river. He found himself grasping at the clothes for support, a lot of small garments.

Suddenly he was facing four little boys in assorted sizes and shades of cream caramel and toffee.

"Hello, Daddy," they said. "Merry Christmas."

He wheeled on the woman, but she had disappeared through the sheets. He heard the door slam behind her. He stared into four pairs of steady black eyes. He tore off his beard.

"What you think?" they said.

"He ain't the right color."

"Mama always say our daddy was light."

"She didn't say he uz this light."

"What is this?" he said. "Who are you?" He couldn't even tell what their nationality was. They might be anything.

They began to snicker and whisper. Finally the youngest said, "We is yo' chirren."

"The hell you are," he told them. He turned and, not without difficulty because of the pants, he beat his way through the sheets and found the door and opened it into the living room. She was nowhere to be seen. He tried the kitchen, the bedroom, the bathroom, and another room with lots of beds. She was gone.

"Mrs. Battersea," he called, but then remembered that her kidneys had gone boom. No answer, but who cared? He was off the hook. Maybe he could rustle up some food from the kitchen for the girls and make a fast getaway.

He reeled past the distant honking of the buzz-buzz-buzzard and back into the bedroom to change his clothes. His pants and his jacket were nowhere to be found. A search produced nothing. She had hidden them, for Chrissake. Or taken them with her. He looked under the bed and felt his Santa trousers going, going, gone. When he turned around, the four kids were lined up in the doorway.

"Daddy" said the youngest, "you is ripped from hell to breakfast."

They gave way before him as he plunged through the door. He tried the door to the hallway and found it locked. He noted that the suitcase he had stumbled on was gone. The boys had followed him. "Get it open," he ordered. "Get the key."

The two oldest in turn tried the knob. "It ain't gonna open, mister. She locked it from outside."

"The hell you say." He felt like the first time in jail they slammed the door.

He backed away, clear back to the TV with a hole in its face, took a running start, and hurled himself against the door. It didn't give, the way it did in television movies. He felt himself bounced backward and slammed into the card table with the dishes from dinner.

He was down. He couldn't move or see. But he could hear them above him.

"He dead."

"Naw, look at 'im breathin'."

"He ain't breathin'."

Then he felt the wine from the glasses on the table running down his face and arm. He was back in the time when he used to catch goldfish with his hand in the bowl. Then he was floating downstream with the laundry. When they pulled him out, there was a catfish in the cabin of his truck. And one in his breast pocket. Then the record came through, drilling into his head: "You'll be so-o-orry you stole my woman. . . ."

He opened his eyes and sat up. He had knocked himself sober. The four boys came and sat around him in a tight semicircle. The youngest, the one they called Cleveland, stuck his finger in the wine, which was running off his shoe, and tasted it and squealed.

Theron struggled to his feet. "Have you got a back door?" When they shook their heads, he checked for himself. There didn't in fact seem to be a back door. He checked the view from all the windows. Then he strode into the back room and tore down all the sheets. He sat on the floor and began knotting them together.

"You gonna fly a kite, mister?" one of them said.

He ignored the question. "When you figger your mother is comin' back?"

They surrounded him again their legs crossed. They shook their heads. "No way a tellin'. She been gone a month."

"Ain' no month."

"She gone a week."

"A month."

"A week."

"Cut it out," he interrupted, standing up to knot his rope. "We got a situation here. Your mama just walked out the door."

They looked up at him and screwed their faces.

"Right?" he said, dragging the sheet rope behind him.

"Wrong," they said, following him. "She ain't our mama. She the sitter," said the oldest, the one they called Woodrow.

They stepped on his rope, and Cleveland fell down when he pulled it away. And out of control, it belted the record player well to his rear and snarled up another reunion in the hay. He lost his cool. "Get up," he yelled, "and tell me where your mama is."

"No way a tellin'. She picked up and lef'."

He reeled in his rope. I been here before, he thought, remembering his wife. This is where I came in. He rubbed his shoulder, which he thought was broken. Then he dragged his rope to the window in the bedroom.

"Mister," said Woodrow right behind him, "I gotta tell it to you straight. Them sheets is in bad shape. They ain't never gonna hold you."

He yanked the rope experimentally and decided it was true. He turned to look down at them. "Will you tell it to me straight? What am I doing here on Christmas Day?"

They twisted their faces. Cleveland said, "We is yo' chirren."

He threw the rope at their feet. He checked the view from the window. To one side he could see a pipe descending. While they watched, he carefully climbed onto the sill and grasped the pipe with both hands. Below him was the pavement about two hundred feet away. Inside, a woman tearfully rejected the Adidas. He wished he had them on.

"You leavin' us?" said Woodrow.

"I'm hopin' to," he said.

He stepped off the sill and began to shinny down the pipe. His pants were shot and the air was cold as hell on his rear. His arm and shoulder hurt. They began to wobble, but he reached the ledge of the window of the floor beneath.

Suddenly a little boy was looking at him through the window with a face of astonishment. Praise the lord, he was raising it. Theron stepped inside. The little kid fell backward and then ran around in circles, yelling, "Mama! Mama! Santy Claus is comin' back! He comin' back!"

A large woman with her head in pink curlers appeared. "What you sayin', boy?" She must have been the one without an ear for music. She stopped when she saw Theron. "Sweet Jesus!" she said. Then she attacked him with a saucepan she was holding. "Shame on you! My boy is a believer. You destroyin' his faith? Get outa here, you bum. I'm callin' the po-lees." And she whacked him on the leg.

He backed into the window and out and up. He could hear her crooning, "Honey, that ain't no Santa. That is some ol' robber. He probably mugged Santa and stole his suit. Did you smell his likker? Santa don't drink." Then the window slammed shut.

The boys helped him inside. "You wasn't long," said Cleveland. "Did you get your business 'tended to?"

He sat on the floor to pull himself together. Again they grouped themselves around him in a pow-wow circle. "We got a little 'baccy you could chew," said one.

"You want us to turn up the music?" said another.

The light outside was getting paler. He looked at his watch, but it seemed to be drowned in plum brandy or whatever. "Let me put it to you straight," he said. "I'm callin' the cops to get me out."

They were motionless before him. Then Woodrow said, "Mister, is you sure you wanta do that?"

He thought about it briefly and decided that he didn't, all things considered, especially his recent history. He inquired as calmly as he could, "You got any idea why she done this to me?"

They looked at one another and screwed up their eyes. "She give us our pick. She say we could have the welfare folks again."

"Pee-yew," the others chorused, holding their noses.

"Or she could advertise in the paper for our sho-nuff papa."

"Look," he said, pleading, "I got to get back. I got two kids at home."

"You got more chirren?" they said, pounding one another in the stomach and head. "Well," they decided, "there ain't no way for you to leave so you better call 'em up and get 'em here."

It took him a while to take this in. His whole right side was now out of commission. He recalled that the rent was due in exactly one week and that his pants had been pinched. "You got food here?" he asked.

"Mister," they said, "you won't believe it." They helped him to his feet and pulled him into the kitchen. At the end was a wooden box, which turned out to be a freezer, and inside it were the most TV dinners he had ever seen in one place. There must have been four hundred. He could hear the woman wailing softly like a police siren in the distance, "Take off your Adidas. . . ."

He leafed through them briefly with his good hand, the left one, and a knowing eye. There were all the old favorites: Mexican Fiesta, Roman Holiday, Southern Sunday, Cape Cod Cookout, Harlem Soul. A few he hadn't come across: Home on the Range and Food for Outer Space. And one called Mork and Mindy, which turned out to be a frozen jigsaw puzzle.

Then it hit him between the eyes. "How we gonna get 'em in?" They laughed fit to kill. "How thick is they?" said Woodrow. "How thick?"

"How thick is yo' chirren?" He measured with his hands.

"About your thick," said Theron.

Then they showed him a loose board behind the freezer and a glimpse of the stairway.

"Where's the telephone?" he asked.

Josephine answered, breathless, "Daddy, when you comin' home?"

"Look, Josephine," he said, "listen carefully. I can't come home because they got me locked in."

He could hear her wailing, "They got Daddy in jail."

"Josephine," he shouted, "get Felicia on the phone."

"Daddy, I told you be careful."

Then Felicia answered, "Daddy? Did you do it again?" She sounded like her mother.

"Look," he said, "I'm not in jail. Get this straight: it isn't jail. Get some clothes together and come to the address you drew a map for. Can you remember how to do it?"

There was a long pause while he heard their whispers and a rustle of paper. They were back in the classified ads, for godsake. But Felicia came on. "Bring our nighties, Daddy?"

"Bring your nighties," he said.

He turned to see the four of them listening with a rapture of attention. Round and round and round went the buzz-buzz-buzzard, stuck in his groove.

"Happy New Year, Daddy-O," Cleveland said.

Deep South Books

The University of Alabama Press